The Epic of Redstone

David Long

Table of Contents

I

The old man sat on the riverbank with his back against a huge log watching the small, clear stream known as the Knife being absorbed by the large, muddy river known as the Smoking River. The Smoking River, called the Missouri by white men, had its beginnings in the snowmelt of the Shining Mountains far to the west. Icy water from the mountains encountering the warm air of the lowlands caused a constant fog to rise from the surface of the river, thus the name, Smoking River.

The swirling patterns made by the clear water from the Knife were constantly changing shape until they gradually disappeared into the muddy water of the larger river. The futile struggle of the small stream for a fleeting second reminded the old man of his own life, which had also been a long, lonely, futile struggle against the overwhelming public opinion in the village in which he lived. And then the thought was gone.

It was a balmy April afternoon and the warm sunshine felt good to the old man's aching bones. Each winter that passed left him just a little weaker, and he knew that he did not have many more such to suffer before he would leave this life. The prospect of dying did not bother him at all. There was only one thing that made this life worth holding on to: his beloved grandson.

He had already lived longer than most of his peers, and it was nearly time to join them in Wanagi Yatu, the place of souls. However, there would not be a single one of them, he was sure, that would be happy to meet him again. They had all considered him eccentric, mainly because he believed with all his heart the epic story that had been handed down through his family from generation to generation for at least five hundred years. Even his son would not believe the story, considering it nothing more than the contriving of some fertile mind far back in the dim past. Only his grandson out of all the people living in the village would listen to him, giving the old man hope that, through the boy, the tradition would be kept alive. The old man prayed that the day would come when someone or some thing would reveal the truth behind the story that meant so much to him.

The old man, and about two thousand other people known as the Numakiki, the People, lived in two villages along the cliff-like banks of the great Smoking River. To the white man, the People were known as the Mandan, a mysterious tribe that showed strong signs of the infusion of white blood sometime in the distant past. The old man himself had the red hair, green eyes, and lightly freck-led skin that were the distinguishing marks of his family, but he also had the large, hooked nose and prominent cheek bones of the native people of the American Plains. Something else that distin-guished him from others in the village: he stood a head taller than the average man.

The Story, to the old man at least, was a personal thing—the living, ongoing history of at least one faction of the People—and it explained much as to why the Mandan were different from the other tribes that lived in the Northern Plains. It seemed as if the People had completely closed their minds to the fact that many of them looked more like white men than Native Americans. They ignored the differences and refused to listen to any attempt to explain them, becoming hostile toward him if he persisted.

He had learned long ago to talk about the past only to those who would willingly listen, and that number dwindled as time went on. The threat of ridicule from the skeptics kept the ones who might have an interest in the Story from talking with the old man. His was a lonely life, but he could no more change his beliefs than the sun could reverse its course. Nearly sixty years as the Story-teller had ingrained the details into his psyche so thoroughly that the epic story had become a part of him. To him at least, the long narrative was the truth; he had no more control over believing it than he had over the beating of his heart.

The great river was running high with melt water from the Shining Mountains and making a soothing, mind-lulling sound as it flowed by. As the old man toyed with the fish-shaped amulet on the rawhide thong worn around his neck, his mind was once again about to drift away into the Time-That-Was-Before when he sensed someone behind him.

"*Hau,* Grandfather. Are you asleep?"

"*Hau,* little one. No, I am simply enjoying the wonderful sunshine that brings warmth to these old, aching bones of mine," said the old man, the love he had for this child plainly visible in his eyes. The boy was twelve years old but tall for his age, taking after his father and grandfather in that respect. He also had the red hair, green eyes, and slightly freckled skin like others of the family. He sat down beside the old man, leaned back against the log, and took the old man's right hand in both of his own, and that is the way they sat for several minutes, silently looking out over the river.

Although the day was warm, the old man was dressed in buckskins and had a woolen blanket, acquired from the white man, around his shoulders. His once muscular frame had become so diminished by age that the now flaccid muscles generated very little warmth. The child wore only a breechcloth and nothing else, not even moccasins. The puppy that was the child's constant companion had wearily plopped down at his feet, without preamble to making a bed, as even puppies are apt to do, and had instantly fallen asleep.

"Were you thinking of the Ancient Ones again, Grandfather? Father says that every time you close your eyes that your mind drifts back into the long ago, into the Time-That-Was-Before. He says that a man cannot live in the long ago, that we can only live in the Time-That-Now-Is. He says that it is a waste of time to give so much consideration to what he calls fables, but I love to hear you tell the Story, Grandfather. I would like for you to start at the very beginning and tell me everything that you remember about the Ancient Ones. Would you please? I love to hear about the strange lands and strange animals that the Ancient Ones owned and about the great canoes driven by the wind and…"

The old man chuckled, but he was immensely pleased that the boy liked to hear the Story, for he believed with all his heart, despite what his son thought, that it was much more than fable. He believed it to be the actual history of an adventurous people long forgotten in time. In the long narrative, the Ancient Ones had crossed the Sunrise Sea, far to the east, in large canoes with wings called sails. Today, everyone knew for a fact that the ancestors of all the white men in this vast land had come from beyond the Sunrise Sea, only much later than the mysterious people in the ancient narrative.

"Yes, little one, my son has closed his mind to that part of his heritage, and if he could, he would deny me the simple pleasure of repeating the tale, especially to you. He must believe it is true, at least in part, or he would not be so vehemently opposed to the telling of it. I suppose he and the rest of the People see the ancient tale as a threat to their accepted beliefs. They want to be the same as all the other tribes around us, but the fact remains that many of us are different. Anyone with eyes to see will have to admit that fact. Personally, I have no problem believing the Ancient Ones actually existed. To me there is no threat at all to the People's beliefs. If they would only listen with an open mind and try to understand, then they too would believe the tale. Everyone knows that the account did not originate with me, that it has been handed down from times farther back than their oldest family members can remember."

"Everyone in the village believes that Lone Man caused men to come forth from the ground, like corn in the springtime. Yet, they shun me for believing that the Creator made man from the dust of the ground, which is the belief handed down from our ancestors, the Norge. Are the two teachings so very different? Is that any reason to treat me as a pariah?"

"Forgive me for rambling. But to answer your question, Grandson, yes, of course, I will be happy to talk of the Ancient Ones, for as long as you want to listen, but I cannot finish the tale in one afternoon. It will take several days, as there is much to tell. Would you not rather be playing with the other boys instead of listening to the ramblings of an old man?"

"No, Grandfather, I have been with my friends all morning. I am tired of playing the same old games. I would much rather listen to you. Start with the Norge before they left their homeland far away to the north and east, please, and tell me everything that you remember."

"You have heard the Story so many times that you could probably tell it to me, couldn't you?"

"I guess so, but I have heard it only in parts, never from beginning to end. I sometimes get confused as to the order of the events. And there are names of people and places that I cannot remember, Grandfather. I will never learn them unless they are repeated to me enough times."

The old man's eyes were glistening with unshed tears from the love he felt for this child. "Yes, of course, you are absolutely right. I can remember how difficult it was for me as a young man to learn all the details. I often wonder just how much of the tale has been forgotten or left out over the many, many years of telling, simply because of strange names and places? There may have been parts dropped for no other reason than sounding too fantastic to believe. Well, there is nothing to be gained by such conjecture. Let's get started then, shall we?"

"I am ready, Grandfather."

"Do you remember the name the Ancient Ones gave the Story?"

"Yes, Grandfather. It is called the Ed-da. Is that, not right?"

"Yes, that is correct. The person who wishes to become the Storyteller must have an excellent memory, and you, Grandson, seemed to be qualified in that respect. That is very important."

"Now, as you already know, the Norge were a hardy people who lived in a cold, mountainous land with thin soil. It is said that the land was so far north that the summer sun was visible even at night. This is something that is beyond my understanding, but it is part of the Ed-da just the same. There are many things in the Ed-da that I have no explanation for; I can only repeat what was told to me. The Norge planted a few vegetables and grains that were hardy enough to mature during the short summers, but they were more dependent on the animals that they kept. They were also successful fishermen, dragging their nets behind the great canoes and hauling dozens of fish at one time from the water."

"Tell me about the strange animals, Grandfather. I like that part of the Ed-da most of all."

The old man laughed. "You probably could tell me what a cow looked like, you little prairie dog, but close your eyes and imagine a wapiti with its many-forked antlers. Then, picture a bison with its two shorter, curved horns. Now, in your mind, remove the antlers and put the bison horns on the wapiti, and that is how a cow was described to me."

After several seconds, the child began to laugh uncontrollably. "What is so funny, you little river otter?" asked the old man, grinning from ear to ear.

"I was imagining what a bison would look like with the antlers of the wapiti on its head," said the boy, and they both laughed until they could laugh no more. To the old man the picture of the bison with antlers really wasn't that funny; he was simply enjoying the laughter of his grandson.

After he could control his laughter, the child said, "Tell me about the sheep, Grandfather, and I promise to be good and not interrupt the Story again."

"Grandson, it is a balm to my soul to laugh with you. That was a very funny image you conjured up; I'll have to admit. Now, the animal called a sheep was more the size of a pronghorn, but it had shorter legs and a heavier body. It had long, curly hair, like the hair on a bull bison's neck and shoulders, covering its body. They were mostly white in color, whereas, the bison is nearly black. The Norge would shear this long hair from the sheep in the springtime and use it to weave warm clothing and blankets, such as this one around my shoulders that was made by the white man. The hair of the sheep would grow long again before winter came. The sheep were also slaughtered for meat, especially the young males. The females were kept for breeding."

"The cows were kept for the milk they produced, as well as for meat. There were other animals called pigs that had flat, tough noses, with which they grubbed in the earth for food. I have never been quite able to picture such an animal in my mind. There is just too little information to go on, and we have nothing with which to compare it. They were closer to the size of sheep than a cow. The pigs were valued for the fat on their bodies as well as their meat. The Story also tells of an animal that men rode upon that could only have been a horse, and you must remember, these animals were mentioned in the Ed-da long before the People had ever seen a horse. It hasn't been so very many years ago that horses were acquired by the People--not so very long before I was born, I would think."

"The Norge were an industrious people and made weapons and tools from metal like the arrowhead that I keep on the string around my neck. This arrowhead, as well as the fish emblem that I treasure, has been passed down for hundreds of years from one Storyteller to the next. Though metal like this is naturally hard, the Norge discovered a method by which they could make it even harder. They guarded this secret well, making their tools and weapons much desired by other people. Trading this metal to other tribes made the Norge very wealthy, and, also, they could clear the land of trees much faster and easier with the harder metal."

"The Norge prospered, and their numbers grew until the land was filled with people. The prairie surrounding our village is so vast that I cannot imagine it ever being filled with people. It is also difficult to imagine a land so covered with trees that they would have to be cut down in order to make farmland, but that is what the Story tells us."

"Will the arrowhead and fish emblem belong to me someday, Grandfather?"

"Yes, Grandson. When one becomes the Storyteller, he also becomes the Keeper of the Emblem. It is nearly time to pass it and the arrowhead on to you. Maybe by the time we finish the Story this time, you will be ready to receive them. They are sacred items that one must never take lightly. You are doing very well, and I am proud of you. I believe you are almost mature enough to become the Keeper. Without your knowledge, my little badger, the Ancient Ones would be totally forgotten after I am gone."

"I love you, Grandfather, please do not talk of going away."

"Nothing but the earth lasts forever, little one, but we will not talk any more of this. Let us get back to the Story."

"The Norge had to have more land in order to support a growing population. To the east and north, the way was blocked by ice. Kindred tribes already occupied the lands to the south. That left only the west in which to expand, and in that direction, there was mostly water—water such as you and I have never seen. This water had a salty taste and was undrinkable, and unlike the river before us, which to us is big, the waters of salt were much too large to see across. It took days of sailing in the giant canoes for the Norge to reach the nearest land to the west. It is said that there were fish in this vast expanse of water that were many times bigger than horses. It is difficult to imagine such creatures, is it not?"

"Some parts of the Story, Grandfather, I promise to learn and remember, but I will reserve judgment on them until later."

"You are wise beyond your years, Grandson. This is what should be done until you have proof, one way or another."

"Having lived for such a long time in a land that bordered on the great salt sea, the Norge learned to build giant canoes, with wings called sails that were woven from the hair of sheep. The wind pushed against these sails, propelling the great canoes forward. The largest of the canoes could carry a hundred or more people. Also, there were great paddles called oars with which to propel the canoes, if need be, but mostly they used the wind when it was blowing favorably. The people would then relax and let the wind do the work for them."

"Would you make a little canoe for me, Grandfather? One with a sail that the wind can push against."

"What happened to the last one that I made for you?"

"The wind stole it away from me. It went far out into the river, and then the current caught it and carried it away. I have never seen it again."

It is said that a great distance to the south this river, the Smoking River, joins with an even greater river called the Father of Waters and that together they flow into the salt sea far, far to the south. If your toy stayed with the current, it could be on its way to a strange land somewhere far across the great salt water." The old man had to smile at the far away look in the child's eyes. What strange images of far away places were forming in his young mind at this moment, he wondered?

When the child came out of his reverie, the old man continued. "The eldest son of a family inherited everything that his father owned, leaving the younger sons to fend for themselves. Banding together these young men became raiders. The Norge were a fierce fighting people, like the Sioux and Pawnee, and at first, they went on raiding forays into other lands--killing, ravaging, plundering, and taking slaves to be sold in other lands. The spoils from these raids, along with the trading of goods to other tribes, helped make them very wealthy. The inhabitants along the coasts of other lands feared the Norge, and in order to pacify some of the raiders, a large number of them were allowed to settle in the lands that they had once plundered. In one of these lands, the native people told the Norge about a large island farther west in the great salt sea that was unpopulated except for a few monks. When news of this island was taken back to their homeland, several large canoes were loaded with animals, tools, and household goods. Sailing west with their wives and children, many of the Norge settled on this island, driving the monks out. And even though there were many fertile valleys covered with grass, and mountain slopes covered with ash and beech, the Norge named the island Iceland."

"Tell me again, Grandfather, what a monk is."

"The part of the Story that I have already told you--from the time that the Norge were raiders until they began to settle down--took place over a long period of time, maybe two hundred years or more. During this time, and even before, the religion of the Norge was called As-a-tru. I do not know the meaning of the word, but I know that they worshipped many gods."

"Well, when the Norge raided in other lands, they encountered a new religion, with only one god, that was spreading throughout all the lands to the west and south. Monks were men who had been converted to the new religion and had decided to dedicate their lives to serving that religion and its One God, the Creator of all things. They lived austere lives separated from other people, especially women, devoting their minds and lives to the new belief. This isolated island, where no one else lived, would have been the perfect place for such a life, if the Norge had not taken it from them. The Norge, themselves, later adopted this new religion as their own."

"What was so different about this new religion, Grandfather?"

"As I said before, the Norge of old worshipped many gods. The new religion had only the one God, the Creator of all things, including men. And he wanted all mankind to be brothers and to love one another and live in peace. Though the One God was Spirit, it is said that he took on flesh and lived among men. Many people believed His teachings, but the leaders of the people rejected Him and killed Him by driving spikes through His hands and feet and leaving Him to hang thus from a tree until He died."

"How was it possible for men to kill a god, Grandfather? Why did He not kill them?"

"It was a demonstration of His love, little one. He allowed this to happen for a reason. After three days, He arose from the grave and appeared to those that believed His teachings. In that way, He proved to them that there is life after the death of the body. He promised the ones that accepted Him as their One God that, though He would leave the earth for a time, His spirit would continue to live in their hearts and be their guide. He also promised that He would someday return to those that believed in Him. I do not know as much as I would like to know about this belief, but in theory at least, it sounds good."

"Our village is peaceful, and the People get along very well with one another. Is that what you mean by being brothers, Grandfather?"

"On a small scale, my child, but I was referring to all men, everywhere. Even at your age, you have some memory of the attack the Lakota made upon our village seven years ago, killing many of our people, don't you? Well, if all men lived as brothers that attack would never have taken place. That our people are peace loving may very well point to the influence of the Norge religion from many, many years ago. Anyway, I like to think that this is so. I, for one, have tried to adhere as much as possible to the idea that all men are brothers."

"But, Grandfather, you have been called Ninekiller since the time of the Lakota attack because you killed nine of their warriors with only a war club as a weapon. It is said that you fought as one possessed. I don't mean to be disrespectful, Grandfather, but how can you kill and still believe in peace?"

"Yes, my child, that is a good question. It is said that I killed nine of the Lakota; I do not know for sure. However, you must understand, there is no contradiction here. Murder and killing in self-defense or in the defense of another are not one and the same. I did what I was forced to do because the Lakota were the aggressors. When I saw your grandmother clubbed to death, I wrested the club from her killer and slew him with it. That is the last thing that I remember until I seemed to awaken from a bad dream after the battle was over. I saw the ground around me littered with the dead and wounded, friend and foe alike. The air was thick with the smell of blood and death. Then I saw the club in my hand, slippery with my blood and the blood of the enemy. I remember flinging the club from my hand and trying to find the body of your grandmother among the dead. That is all that I remembered until the next day."

"What others tell me about the battle is all that I know. When I awoke the next morning, my legs would not support my weight. I had never been so weak and sore before in my life. Every muscle in my body was aching. There were wounds and bruises over my entire body. Many of the scars are still visible. I have never completely recovered my strength from that day. Even though I had lived for more than sixty winters before the battle took place, my body was like the body of one ten years younger; but in that single day, I became an old man. A great deal of my desire to live died with your grandmother. Soon I shall see her again," he said with a wistful smile.

"If one kills in self-defense or in the defense of another there is no wrong done. The wrong is with the aggressor. Everyone has the right to protect himself and his friends and loved ones. I was fighting to save the lives of my family, including you, my little one. If all peace-loving people refused to defend themselves, how long do you think they would last? If the Lakota had met no resistance that day, they would have killed all our warriors and taken the women and children as prisoners and slaves. I would be dead, and you would be a Lakota, living in a tipi. The *Numakiki*, as a separate people, would have ceased to exist. Others named me Ninekiller; it is not a name of my choosing, but I am not ashamed of it. I would do the same thing again, if necessary."

14

"It is said that because of your courage that day, the other warriors took heart and the Lakota were soundly defeated, Grandfather. I am proud to be your grandson."

"I wish it was for some other reason that you are proud, Grandson, but as I said, I am not ashamed of the stand I made against the enemy that day. The loss of your Grandmother, though, is something that I have never recovered from."

"Now, to get back to the Story. Because there were no predators living on the island of Iceland, it was the perfect place to raise sheep and cows. More and more people sailed from Norgeland and settled on the island until all the best land was taken, but fortunately, yet another land was discovered even farther to the west. All this newly discovered land, except for the extreme southern tip, was covered with ice. Do you remember what the Norge called this land?"

"Greenland! That is peculiar isn't it, Grandfather? The land with trees and grass was called Iceland, and the land of ice was called Greenland."

"Yes. If Greenland had been discovered first, maybe the names would have been reversed. The man who discovered Greenland wanted, by giving the land an attractive name, to entice others to go there and settle. There was plenty of grass in Greenland, but it was too cold for trees to grow to a size large enough to be very useful. Enough fodder could be gathered in the summertime to feed the animals all winter, and the animals and people thrived for many, many years. Over the years, there came to be more Norge living in Greenland than there are people presently living in our two villages."

"Why was there so much ice in this new land, Grandfather?"

"Well, my little fox kit, it is common knowledge that the farther north one goes the colder it gets. The opposite is true in the other direction—the farther south, the warmer it gets, but I cannot tell you why. I am convinced, however, that the sun plays a major role in this. As you know, when the sun travels to the south in the winter, the cold comes blowing in from the north. The snows come and the ground freezes and all creatures try to find shelter. The great bison herds that pass by every autumn migrating to the south presumably are seeking a warmer climate with better forage. In the spring of course, they return to the north."

"There are stories that have been passed on to us from the Algonquin tribes to the north about a race of people even farther to the north who live all their lives on ice, hunting animals that live on and under the ice. The Ice Dwellers of Greenland, also called Eaters of Raw Flesh, are also mentioned in the Ed-da. Personally, I question the accuracy of such tales. How would it be possible for animals to live under the ice? What would they eat?"

"If you don't know, Grandfather, you can be certain that I don't know."

The old man smiled. "It really wasn't a question that I expected you to answer, my child. Could it be that the story about the Norge sounds just as farfetched to our people as the Ice Dweller tale does to me?"

"Parts of the Story are rather fantastic, Grandfather. I think you will have to admit that."

"Yes, especially the parts that can't be explained, but as a whole, it makes so much sense, if one would but listen to the entire story with an open mind. Anyway, the Norge lived in Greenland for three hundred and more years and prospered for most of that time. During their sojourn there, explorers from Greenland sailed even farther west across the Sunrise Sea and found yet another land, another large island. This newfound land, a part of our own vast land, I believe, was already occupied by a race of people that the Norge called Skraelings, meaning savages or barbarians."

"The Skraelings, for some unknown reason, painted their entire bodies red. The Norge sometimes referred to them as red men, a name that has been transferred to all the original inhabitants of this vast land, including us, even though, as anyone can see, we are not red."

"The Norge explorers built a village of several earth-covered lodges, such as the ones we live in, on the newfound island, but the constant fighting with the Skraelings caused the Norge to abandon the village and return to Greenland. However, during the time they lived in the newfound land, the Norge explored the surrounding area and found a vast, bountiful land, again to the west. They were so impressed with the amount of wild grapes growing there that they named the place Vineland. This land was also occupied by Skraelings."

"Even though they were forced to abandon their village on the island, the Norge never forgot about the land of grapes. They kept the memory alive through stories just as you and I are doing at this moment. That particular group was forced to return to Greenland, but other attempts were made to colonize the newfound land even farther to the west. From the time the Norge left their homeland in the east, their explorations always took them farther and farther to the west."

"You and I had better return to the lodge, little one. The sun is going down, and my stomach is complaining about being ignored since dawn. Your mother probably has a delicious stew waiting for us. We will take up the Story again tomorrow if you wish."

It was already getting dark inside the lodge by the time they finished eating. The stew was nowhere close to being delicious, as Ninekiller knew even before he took the first bite. The bison meat harvested last autumn was all gone, so it would be dog or jackrabbit stew for the rest of the summer. A young pronghorn would be welcome fare, but his son had never been adept at hunting, and besides, he was lazy. Well, he wouldn't complain. Since he was too old to earn his keep, he would have to eat whatever was available. Besides, the maize, beans, and squash would be ripening in a few weeks. The thought of fresh boiled maize made his mouth water.

Until he lay down, he hadn't realized that he was so tired. As he lay on his bed looking at the stars through the smoke hole in the center of the roof, Ninekiller could not help but wonder if the Norge were the original designers of the earth covered lodges that the People lived in. He knew from the Story that the Norge built earth lodges in the newfound land. Of all the Plains tribes, only the Mandan, Arikara, and Hidatsa built such large permanent houses, and the other tribes that built anything similar could have copied the design from the Mandan. Most of the other Plains tribes lived in portable lodges of skins and poles, called tepees. The Pawnee people to the south built lodges, but much smaller and of a totally different design than the Mandan lodges. To him, at least, the earth lodges were another link to the Norge.

II

The rising sun, peeking over the eastern horizon and illuminating a cloudless sky, promised another beautiful day. Ninekiller forced himself to eat another portion of the tasteless stew for breakfast. He had not really enjoyed eating since he had lost his beautiful wife, Catkin. Now there was a real cook! Catkin could have given oak leaves a mouthwatering flavor. His daughter-in-law was no better at cooking than his son was at hunting. What was the younger generation coming to anyway? Already, they were so dependent on the white man's trade goods that they could make almost nothing for themselves anymore. However, he would have to admit, though reluctantly, that steel knives and guns were superior to flint arrows and bows, and copper kettles were better than boiling skins and hot rocks.

The rest of the family were beginning to awaken as he left the lodge to make his way back to his favorite spot by the river to wait for his grandson. The triangle of land at the junction of the two rivers was his favorite place to sit, think, and pray. It was sufficiently far from the village to ensure a certain amount of privacy, and the big log made a good backrest. A nearby willow tree, planted years ago by his own hands, provided shade when the sun became too hot during summer afternoons. He finished his daily prayer to the rising sun before the full orb cleared the horizon. Although he believed in the One God of the Norge, his reverence for the sun had never diminished. Without the sun, there would be no life on the earth.

The great log was once a mighty oak tree that stood at the edge of the high riverbank, leaning away from the river as if in fear of what someday would happen. After every spring flood, the river undercut the roots of the tree ever so slowly, until there was no more purchase to hold it upright. And then one spring afternoon during a thunderstorm, a heavy gust of wind blew the tree down. To obtain firewood the villagers attacked the tree with hatchets until there was nothing left but the main trunk. The old man almost immediately claimed the log as his own private sanctuary, and had, over a period of many months, sat in the same spot so many times that he had worn a formfitting depression in the ground. He was there every morning, weather permitting, to greet the rising sun and to pray to the One God.

Prying a piece of bark from the log, he began to shape it into the form of a canoe. Drilling a hole through the center of the bark with the point of his knife, a steel knife made by white men, he inserted a cattail stalk for a mast. There were no leaves mature enough this early in the year to use as a sail, so a square of stiff leather would have to suffice. Making two holes in the piece of skin, he slipped the cattail through the holes, and the toy was finished. Sitting down with his back against the log, he placed the toy by his left side. It had taken most of an hour to make the canoe, but it was still early. Ferret would still be playing for a while yet. He closed his eyes and let his mind drift back to the days of his youth. He could remember most of his younger years as if they were only yesterday. He had been happy as a young man; there was nothing about that part of his life that he would change, even if he could.

A smile tugged at the corners of his mouth when he thought about the first time that he had really looked at Catkin. Since both of them had lived all their lives in the same village, he had seen her almost daily. But suddenly it seemed as if she wasn't the same little girl with a figure like a stick anymore. Her hips were getting wider, and her chest was expanding quite nicely; she was really a very pretty girl. Even now, he could feel the blush that had reddened his face when she had caught him staring at her. When she had smiled at him, he had quickly looked at the ground and walked away. It was at least a month before he could muster enough courage to speak to her—a whole month in which he could think of nothing else but her beautiful smile. Oh, he missed her so much.

Ninekiller hadn't realized that his smile had turned to tears until he heard Ferret laughing. The boy thought the antics of the fat little puppy, which was almost as round as a ball, were hilarious as it struggled to keep pace with him. The old man quickly wiped his eyes with the back of his hands and put on a smile to greet his grandson.

"Good morning, Grandfather. How are you today? Have you been here long?"

"Yes. A while. There was something I wanted to do before we started on the Story once again," said the old man, as he presented the toy canoe to the child.

"Ooh!" Exclaimed the boy. "Thank you, Grandfather. I will be more careful with this one," said Ferret, as he admired the toy.

"Now where did we get to with the Ed-da? Do you remember, little one?"

"Yes, Grandfather. The Norge had to abandon their village in the newfound land and sailed back to Greenland."

"Yes, of course. Well, as far as I know there were no more attempts to permanently colonize the newfound island to the west, although there were other areas in the new land that were explored, some not so far from this very village, it is said. The vastness and richness of the new lands, though, was something that was never forgotten by the people living in Greenland. The Norge continued to live and prosper in Greenland for probably two hundred years after the abandonment of the island village. Then for some unknown reason, the weather in Greenland began to grow colder. The snow began to melt later and later in the spring, and the cold came earlier in the autumn, making the summers too short for grass to grow tall, as it once had. It became harder and harder to gather enough fodder to feed the animals through the winter. Sometimes it would snow even in the summertime. The seas were dotted with huge chunks of floating ice, and great storms would blow in from the north, making fishing on the seas very dangerous."

"The people began to eat more of their animals than were being born. At first, this was not so noticeable, but as the number of animals began to dwindle, some of the people became alarmed. They ate the dogs early on for obvious reasons. Some believed the cold to be temporary and conditions would improve in time, but others began to make preparations to leave. There were not enough of the giant canoes to carry all the people away from Greenland, but those that could, sailed east to Iceland. The people that were left began to worry more about the future. The food supply was greatly diminished, and there was no way to make the remaining food last beyond a certain point. Some rescue attempts were launched from Iceland but were halted when storms and ice made conditions too perilous to continue."

Some of the Greenlanders knew that death awaited them not many years into the future, if they did nothing. There were two separate populated areas on the island, the Eastern and Western Settlements. The Eastern Settlement fared much better than its counterpart in the west. One particular giant of a man, with a great red beard, named Steinn the Red, our ancestor, called together a council of all the adult males in the Western Settlement to discuss the situation. They met in the largest house of worship in the colony, but even then, there was little room to spare, forcing some to stand throughout the meeting."

"Opinions differed as to what should be done to meet the impending doom that was sure to come if conditions did not change for the better. There were still those that wanted to do nothing but wait, but Steinn was not one of them. His own plan was to build as many canoes as possible from the limited materials available and sail west to the newfound land and try again to live among the Skraelings. Everyone knew that the lands in the west were vast and bountiful; the lands in the east were already taken. That is the reason their ancestors had left in the first place, Steinn argued. If they sailed back to Iceland or Norgeland, where would they find land to settle on?"

"Do you remember what Steinn means, little one?"

"It means stone, doesn't it, Grandfather?"

"That's right, it means stone. Steinn the Red could also be called Red Stone."

"As the meeting continued, the chief priest of the Western Colony became involved in the discussion. He wanted the situation to remain the same, telling the people that anyone who left Greenland to live among the Skraelings would be excommunicated from the One God religion. This statement infuriated Steinn, who had great faith in the One God, but had little respect for the religious leaders, who took their living from the people they were supposed to serve."

"Tell me again what a priest is, Grandfather."

"Do you remember the monks you asked about yesterday who were the first people to live in Iceland? Well a priest is a man who has also dedicated his life to the service of the believers, but instead of living a secluded life, he lived among the common people and served as their religious leader. The closest comparison in our village would be our shaman, who performs religious rites for the People. Now, to be excommunicated was to be condemned to a place called hell, where the soul would be tormented forever. To most believers this was the most fearful threat that they could possibly face, and they would avoid excommunication at almost any cost."

"Steinn, who was normally reserved in religious matters, was lost in his anger toward the priest. 'Do you dare threaten us with excommunication after the way you priests have slowly taken our very livelihood away from us,' he thundered. 'For many years we have suffered at the hands of the priesthood. Everyone has been afraid to say anything for fear that this very thing would happen, but we are to the point of starvation. You priests charge such exorbitant fees for christenings, baptisms, weddings, and other rites that we are now slaves of the Church. The Church owns nearly everything, while we are practically destitute. It is difficult enough to eke out a living as it is without you priests sucking our lifeblood from our bodies. It is time for a change. We even have to buy the right to go fishing. It is time to be free men or die trying. You priests, and anyone else who chooses, can remain here and freeze or starve as you please. As for me, I am leaving this sorry life, this freezing land, and as soon as possible. Anyone who wishes can go with me,

24

as long as there is room in the ship that I intend to build.' With that, he turned and left the stunned listeners, their mouths agape. They could hardly believe that the grievances they had harbored in silence for so long had finally been aired."

"Steinn began immediately to act on his plan by tearing the best timbers and boards from the houses abandoned in the past few years by those who had already returned to the east. Since it was winter, it would be necessary to keep his own dwelling intact until springtime. He sometimes had to transport for some distance the timbers from the abandoned houses before sawing them into boards to build the great canoe. He and his horse were never idle while there was light enough to see. Since there were no trees in Greenland, some of the logs he used had been brought from Iceland or Vineland many, many years before. Now, after many decades of cutting, the forests of Iceland were almost depleted. The first explorers to the newfound land to the west had also returned to Greenland with boatloads of timbers, and at least one voyage had been made, only a few years past, to Markland to the west for more timber. Wood was a valuable commodity in a land with no trees."

"Steinn was lucky to have gotten a head start on his neighbors. When news of what he was doing circulated throughout the community, some of his friends came to see the great canoe taking shape. The structure was about fifty feet long and would be of shallow draft, so that it could be easily beached. Many of the other men who were handy with tools saw in Steinn's craft the feasibility of escaping from certain starvation and begged to help with the construction of it. Steinn put some of his friends to sawing boards and others to making timber bolts from scrap metal. Those of a more independent nature began to salvage every suitable timber, from whatever source available, to start building their own canoes."

"It soon became apparent that every family could not gather enough material to have its own personal ship. Much of the timber was unsuitable for use, being too short, or too crooked, or too small in diameter. Another meeting was scheduled, only this time without the priests, to discuss the problem. It was decided to pool the scattered wood and use the best timbers in the construction of another ship being built by an experienced sailor named Floki. After a lengthily discussion no further resolution was forthcoming, so the men left the meeting in low spirits."

"Soon, the only heavy timbers left were in the houses of worship, buildings considered sacred that had stood for many years. Everyone had great respect for these buildings, but the timber would better serve in the construction of a ship, to save lives, than in a place of worship, especially since there would soon be no one but the priests left to attend the worship services. At least that was the reasoning of those needing the wood."

"A great dispute concerning the use of the timbers arose between the priests, who intended to stay in Greenland, and the people wanting to escape. All the priests could do was threaten the people with excommunication, but the hope of a new life in the West was stronger than their fear of the priests. Raids were made under the protection of darkness and the timbers in the houses of worship soon disappeared. In all, there were three great canoes built from the salvaged wood. Some of the boards were so narrow that the canoes had to be built double walled. This type of construction took twice as many boards, but on the other hand it required less pine tar, an item in short supply in this land without trees. It took months to build the ships, but finally the little fleet was ready to sail, yet the fact remained that there would not be enough room aboard three ships for all the people, and their supplies, too."

If the problem couldn't be solved, the three new ships could be used to transfer timber from Markland to construct more ships or to take half of the people to Vineland, thus requiring two dangerous voyages across the icy sea necessary. Steinn didn't like either prospect. Surely there must be another way.

"One particularly fine day, Steinn was standing on a promontory looking out to sea and going over in his mind the route taken by the earlier explorers to the new land, when the solution to the problem flashed into his mind. He was so excited that he ran to his nearest neighbor shouting at the top of his lungs. The man was so startled that he answered with a sword in his hand, the loud, insistent knock at his door. Steinn was almost incoherent as he insisted that another meeting be convened immediately."

"It took at least an hour for word to circulate throughout the scattered farms, by which time Steinn had calmed down, but he refused to divulge his reason for calling the meeting until all were present. They were gathered inside the bare rock walls of a former house of worship, the wood having been taken months ago. The walls were useful only as a windbreak, but the meeting wouldn't have to be a long one."

"Do any of you remember in the written accounts of the voyages of discovery to Vinland how one of our ancestors, returning to Greenland, came upon a shipwreck on the island of Heluland just a short distance across the strait from here?" Steinn began. There was a general nodding of heads. "The shipwrecked crew was rescued and brought home, but the ship and the cargo of logs from Markland, were left behind. The captain of the rescue vessel then sailed back across the strait, salvaged what he could of the wrecked ship, made a raft of the logs, and towed them here."

It was generally agreed that was what happened, but no one seemed to grasp as yet the point that Steinn was trying to make. "We have lots of wood that is unsuitable for shipbuilding, but it will float", said Steinn. "Why not make three rafts that can be towed to Vinland behind our three ships? We can easily fit everyone into the ships and load the rafts with our belongings. It would be slow going, and maybe even dangerous, since the ships would be less maneuverable, but there is no reason that I can think of why it wouldn't work." The men were ecstatic! Not a soul dissented, so the plan was adopted, and the construction of the rafts got under way. Since he was the only one to have shown any leadership ability, Steinn was unanimously elected leader of the colony.

The route to the new land and the approximate time it would take was already known from previous voyages. It had been decided that the expedition would be launched at the first of June; thereby, giving them time to make the voyage to the new land and to make preparations for the next winter. Slaughtering the remaining animals and preserving the meat for the voyage was begun immediately. Altogether, there were approximately three hundred and fifty men, women, and children—of that number one hundred and fifty were males fourteen years and older--that would be sailing away from the only home that they had ever known."

"There was much resentment from the priests toward those that were planning to leave. The majority of the people would have preferred to remain in good grace with the priests, but it was not possible. One cold, windy night, when nearly everyone was asleep, there was an unsuccessful attempt to burn one of the canoes. Luckily, the fire was discovered and doused before much damage was done. Everyone felt that one of the priests had made the attempt, but there was no actual proof. From that time until the ships were launched, a constant guard was maintained to protect them."

"Since the long smoldering resentment toward the priests had finally been vocalized, many of the men, with the instigation of Floki, were now willing to go so far as to take punitive action against them, at least to put them under armed guard, but Steinn declined to go that far. After the ships sailed, Steinn figured, the Ice Dwellers would come down from the north and slaughter the priests, or they would slowly starve. That would be punishment enough."

"The weather warmed to the point that Steinn decided to launch the voyage, during the middle of May. Since everything that was to be taken had already been gathered, the rafts were quickly loaded and before dawn, the people went aboard the ships. Since very little metal would be available in the new land, every nail and scrap of iron and brass that could be found had been taken aboard."

"As the ropes holding the great canoes were loosed, many of the women on board, knowing that they would never see their homeland again, began to cry with a loud wail, alerting the priests asleep inside their dwellings. The men began to pull harder at the oars to put more distance between them and the shore. The priests ran down to the seashore, shaking their fists and hurling vicious curses and threats at the ones that were leaving. The curses and threats came too late; the voyageurs were safely on their way."

"I will see you in hell, Steinn," shouted the chief priest.

"I am sure you will, you sanctimonious fee grabber, for you will probably be there ahead of me," Steinn shouted back.

"You know that is not what I meant, you spawn of the devil," the priest cried. Steinn turned his back and faced the open sea. What was to be gained by hurling insults at a man he actually pitied?

"The plan was to sail directly to the southwest across the open sea rather than take the longer island-hopping route to the north, then west, and finally south. They hoped to find seas with fewer ice floes by taking this more southerly route, then when land was sighted, to sail south along the shore until they came to the island of Vinland."

"Before they were beyond the sight of land, the ships were drawn close together so that Steinn could lead the people in prayer to the One God, asking for a safe voyage to the new lands. The sails were then hoisted, and soon Greenland was left behind. They had to be constantly alert because of the floating ice, but as was expected, the farther south and west they sailed the more the sea opened up, making the ice more scattered."

"The three giant canoes were closely packed with people, but with the cargo being stored on the rafts, the voyage was bearable. Little cooking had to be done at sea, the women having prepared food before leaving Greenland. If it became necessary to retrieve an item from a raft, the sail of the towing ship would be furled, and the ship would be maneuvered by oar along beside the raft. To be safe, all three ships were kept within sight of each other. When fog was encountered, the blowing of ram's horns kept the ships within hearing distance of each other"

The drag created by the rafts made the crossing slower than normal, evoking complaints from a few who were afraid the ships had gone off course, but on the morning of the eleventh day, land was sighted. After they had found a safe landing place in a small, sheltered cove, Steinn led the people in a prayer of thanksgiving. The voyage, except for the constant threat of ice, had been uneventful."

"Grandfather, I have a question that I have never asked before—that I never even thought of before. How could Steinn keep the canoes on course in the fog, or if there happened to be clouds, and he couldn't see the sun or the stars at night?"

"That is an excellent question, and it shows that you have a very sharp mind, my little prairie chicken. It is time, I should think, to show you the secret that is always been passed on to the Keeper of the Fish Emblem. That question tells me that you are ready to become the Keeper. If you will go and fetch a long hair from the mane or tail of a horse, I will reveal the secret to you. Do not stand behind the horse when you pull the hair," the old man warned.

"I know better than to do that, Grandfather. I am not a little child anymore."

Ferret quickly placed the toy canoe on the log and ran as fast as possible, followed by the puppy, toward the nearest horses. He ran so fast that the puppy couldn't keep up the pace; whereas, it sat down on its haunches, lifted its nose skyward, and let go a plaintive howl. When that got the puppy no attention, it began to cast about for the boy's scent. Within seconds, the boy came running back just as fast as he had left. Seeing a figure hurtle past, the puppy was so startled that it yelped in surprise and fell sideways on its side, then recognizing its master, trotted clumsily back to the log and plopped down.

Ninekiller had taken the fish emblem from the rawhide cord while waiting for Ferret's return. Taking the hair, he tied one end of it through the hole in the back of the emblem. By the loose end of the hair, he held the emblem in the air so that it would be free to rotate.

"Do you know which way is north, Grandson?" asked the old man. Ferret unhesitatingly pointed in the right direction. "That's right. Now, I am going to point the head of the fish toward the east. Now, see how the fish slowly turns to point north? Now, I'll turn it in the opposite direction. See how it again turns to the north? I am going to turn it all the way around to the south. It takes a while longer before it comes to a complete stop, but it still points to the north. Here, you try it," said the old man, as he handed the emblem to the boy.

"Remember, it must always be tied with a limber string—rawhide will not work. There is another way to do it without a string. The emblem can be placed on a piece of bark or wood chip just big enough to float it, but the water must be still, and the bark cannot be allowed to contact anything. Never try that method in the river; the emblem could very easily be lost that way, just as your first toy canoe was lost.

"There is one more thing that I want to show you about the fish emblem. This metal arrowhead and the fish are attracted to each other. Watch what happens when they come close to one another," said Ninekiller, after he had tied half of the horsehair to the arrowhead. Holding a string in each hand, the objects, after passing a certain point, seemed to leap toward each other and cling. Then he laid the fish emblem on the ground and touched it with the blade of his knife. The emblem clung to the knife and could be lifted off the ground.

"Grandfather? By what magic does the emblem work? Did the Norge put a spell on it?"

"That is something that I do not know. I only know that it works. That is how the Norge could find their way across the great waters. With this stone in your possession, you can never get lost." Putting the emblem back on the thong, he slipped it over Ferret's head. "I am now entrusting the emblem to you. It is of great age; treat it with reverence."

"I will, Grandfather. I promise. Grandfather? What happened to the priests that remained in Greenland? Did the weather turn warm again or did they starve?"

"I have no definite answer for that question, little one. When the great canoes left for the new lands, all contact with Greenland was broken. I hope someone from the Eastern Colony rescued them, but I cannot say one way or the other. After Steinn and the others arrived in Vinland, there was no return voyage to Greenland; they continued their way toward the west."

"After the safe landing in what was believed to be Markland, so named by the earlier explorers because of the forests, they followed the coastline southward and had little trouble locating the ancient village once occupied by those explorers. The mounds, left where the earth-covered lodges had stood, were set back from the sea, but were easily seen across a shallow bay. A small brook of cold, clear water ran through the meadow close by the ancient village. The lodges, now three hundred years old, were in un-repairable condition. All of them had collapsed and were of no use, whatsoever, as shelters. The new arrivals would have to make other provisions for winter lodges. They planned to be here only one cold season at most, and at this southern latitude their shelters could be far less elaborate than the ones in Greenland's colder climate."

"The bay was so shallow that at low tide the ships could not anchor near the shore where the village was located. After the tide came in, they were rowed up the brook and anchored. The rafts were moored close at hand so they could be dismantled as needed.

"Explain to me once again about tides, Grandfather."

"It is the rising of the sea at certain times and the receding at other times. The reason for this is just one more thing that has no explanation in the Ed-da. I do so wish that as a young man I had visited the great salt sea in the east or south. There are so many mysteries in the Story that might have been made clearer with even a little exploration," said the old man, with a wistful look in his eyes.

"As the people worked to get established in the new land, all contact with the Skraelings was kept on friendly terms by order of Steinn. If troubles did arise, he wanted his people to be innocent of all wrongdoing. The Norge were now strangers in a strange land, he said, and if they were to survive, they could not afford to make enemies among the native population. He believed that lack of respect for the natives was the reason for the failure of the earlier colonists. According to the Ed-da, the earlier explorers for no reason killed several Markland Skraelings while they were under their canoes asleep on the beach. That incident got the leader of the explorers killed in retaliation. There were a few grumblers in Steinn's group who looked upon the Skraelings with scorn, the man called Floki being the most notable, but no one dared to openly oppose Steinn. He was a head taller than any of the other men and known to have a fiery temper when riled."

"The first half of summer was spent building new lodges, gathering berries, hunting, and fishing. The little stream that meandered by the village, as well as the small lake it drained, glistened with salmon. The food stores were growing fast and before the first snows arrived, there should be more than enough dried fish and meat to see them through the winter. Since no domesticated animals had been brought to the new land, the gathering of fodder for the winter was not necessary, but without cows, there was no milk—the one thing everyone seemed to miss most. Someone soon discovered that caribou antlers when boiled long enough would eventually take on the consistency of butter, and when salted, could be used as a substitute for that food."

All the first week everyone available removed stones from the old lodge sites to be used in the new shelters. The rafts were dismantled, the wood being used in the construction of the new homes. Even the children were kept busy hauling containers of soil. When the new sites were made ready, the men began bringing saplings from the nearby hills to make the house frames. The women and children dumped soil on top to cover the new lodges. In three weeks, the last lodge was ready for occupation.

"While most of the people had been occupied with preparations for winter, one ship, under the leadership of Floki Magnusson, was sent to the west to explore the coastline. Floki, a charismatic man of less than average height and weight, was a capable leader of men, but his independent attitude often caused conflict. Floki's crew, which was more loyal to him than to Steinn, consisted only of young adventurous men.

At Steinn's direction, they were to sail west, keeping the shore to portside, looking for a passage to the south into the interior of the land. They sailed hundreds of leagues to the west and never reached the end of the new land. Surely, Floki thought, this land was too vast to be a single island; it had to be an unknown continent, or at least a series of very large islands. Many wonders were seen, but no passage to the south was found. Sailing south on the open sea was possible, but the shore in that direction was always to starboard."

"When Floki returned after weeks of exploring, he brought back glowing tales of a land covered with giant oaks and hickories and filled with wild game. Nuts and berries abounded, and fish were plentiful. This had to be the Vinland of the earlier explorers, because of the abundance of vines, but it was too early in the year for ripe grapes to be found, anywhere."

"That evening a meeting of the adult males was called, so that all could hear the results of Floki's explorations. They met in the center of the new village, where a large fire was kept burning to give off light. Steinn ordered that all weapons be left in the shelters. If tempers flared, havoc could reign in such a large gathering. It had happened many times before, even in his own family. Thorvald, the father of Eric the Red, one of Steinns forefathers, was expelled from Norgeland for killing a man during a dispute. Years later, Eric himself was expelled from Iceland for the same reason. The Norge, as a people, were often too quick to settle differences with violence. While they were yet in Greenland, the priests were a mollifying influence, but here, in this wild new land, Steinn was the only person with any authority. He intended to play it safe."

"After everyone was seated and quieted, Floki was asked to give his account of the explorations. Steinn did not particularly like the man, but he had to admit, Floki was a capable leader and sailor. There had already been subtle signs that Floki would like to be the leader of all the Norge, or at the very least be the leader of a sizable splinter group. This was one man that Steinn was determined to keep an eye on. He intended to keep the whole party together, if at all possible. There was strength in numbers. Separated, they would be easy prey for any enemy."

"Grandson, let us pretend that we are there among the crowd and can hear Floki as he gives his speech. Close your eyes and listen as if I were Floki as he describes the voyage and the new lands that he has seen," said Ninekiller, as he sank a little lower and laid his head back against the log.

The fire is blazing brightly as Floki stands in the center of the gathering. The faces of the men glow orange from the reflected light. The eyes of the listeners follow his every move as Floki begins his narration. "Fourteen days sailing to the west at the end of a great estuary, there is a large freshwater lake, teeming with fish. At the entrance to this lake are many small islands; any one of them would be an ideal place for a fortified village That could be easily defended. A few leagues up the river gorge feeding this huge lake is the grandest waterfall that any of us had ever seen. It is magnificent, and the roar of the falling water sounds like constant thunder. It is a much better land than the one we now occupy. Fish and game abound. There are mighty oaks and beech--every kind of tree—just waiting for our axes. And the soil…the soil is the darkest, richest that I have ever seen. I am sure that crops would grow without any fertilization at all."

"Some of us climbed around the great falls and there before us was another lake, as big as the first, as big as a sea. There was no contact made with Skraelings, but we found campsites that had been recently occupied. And there is a portage trail to the top of the falls. We found signs that canoes, too heavy to carry, had been dragged along this trail. It would be possible, I am sure, with a little hard work, to haul our ships up this trail to the lake above the falls. Who knows how far one could explore into the interior of this vast land?"

"Come spring," continued Floki, "I would like nothing better than to lead a group back to the first lake and build a permanent settlement on one of the islands. Are there any volunteers who would like to go with me?"

At this time, Steinn took the floor. "Before any of you make any hasty decisions, remember that I am still the elected leader of this expedition. It was my idea to leave Greenland in the first place. There will be no splintering of this party as long as I am the leader. Now, I have something to show you," as he reached inside his shirt and drew out a folded paper, yellow with age, wrapped in leather. "This document has been the property of my family for generations. Though I cannot say for certain, it is purported to have belonged to Leif Eriksson himself. He was one of my ancestors, as you all know. It tells of an early exploration into the lands to the west of Greenland. Regretfully, there was no map included with the document, making the places mentioned rather vague at best. However, if I find any of the landmarks mentioned, I am sure that I will recognize them."

"The previous explorers sailed west to Heluland, then south to Markland, and then on to Vinland. But we sailed southwest directly to Markland to shorten our voyage and to avoid the ice before turning south. By my reckoning, that should have put us at the same destination as the first explorers, but the description of the land that Floki has explored does not match what is written in this document. The ruins of the earth houses prove that someone lived here once, but we don't know whom. The writer of this document only says that the land described lies far to the west. He describes a land of grass as tall as a man where great herds of bison roam. These animals were so numerous that it took days for a herd to pass by. No one would ever go hungry in such a land as this. It has been my life-long dream to find this particular land, and I will settle in another place, only as a last resort."

"That is totally unbelievable!" exclaimed Floki. "Who could be expected to accept such a story? What I have told you about, I have seen with my own eyes, but I saw no place that even comes close to what you described. This whole land--north, west, and south--is covered with forests, not grass. We should take what I personally know we could have--not put our hope in some fantasy land."

"Let me have my say before you discount this document as a fake," Steinn demanded. "All the people who sailed in the earlier explorations, as we know, did not return to Greenland. Many remained to make their homes here. There could be a growing colony of our people somewhere in this new land--if we can only find it. Now, I took for granted that they sailed west and then south which would have brought them here to this location, but I could be in error."

"Now, listen while I tell you what the chronicle says, and maybe, together, we can come to some conclusion as to the location of this land. The writer says that after sailing through the western passage, the shoreline was always to the port side as they made their way southward along the shore of an inland sea. Now, Floki, at my request, kept the shore on the port side as he sailed west, but he found no place to turn to the south. The great lakes, as big as seas that he found, were of fresh water. The writer of the chronicle says that he sailed on a salt water sea."

"Taking it for granted that the early explorers sailed west from this old village, could be my big mistake. After thinking about it, I now believe they must have sailed directly west from Greenland. If there is a passage somewhere to the north of here that would allow one to sail even farther to the west, then we missed it on the voyage over by sailing too far to the south. If there is a passage, it must be between Heluland and Markland. If Markland is a huge island, and we can find a way to the other side, that would set everything right. We would then be able to sail southward on the back side of Markland with the shore on the left side."

"The summer is barely more than half over. I propose that we send a ship to the north along the coast of Markland to search for this passage to the west. We should not be too hasty in choosing a site for a permanent settlement. Since we can't possibly leave this place until spring, why not do more exploring before winter comes?"

"Who would want to live in a land with nothing but grass, when there is such an excess of trees all around us? What would we use to build lodges? How could we make bows and spears, or anything that requires wood?" asked Floki, more than a little agitated.

"You lived in Greenland your whole life where there were no plants that were worthy of being called trees. Besides, according to the account, the grasslands border on forests. That is where some of the earlier travelers settled, at the fringe of the forest. They had access to timber as well as the great herds of bison. There were numerous small lakes in the area, teeming with fish," said Steinn. With this argument, the wind seemed to go out of Floki's sails. Steinn had won a small victory, but he knew that the war was far from over."

"Floki, you are the natural choice to command such a voyage of exploration, but if you refuse, I will understand. You have spent half the summer on the sea already, if you would like to sit this one out, just say so," said Steinn, though he had no idea whom he could trust with such a task if Floki turned it down."

"I was born to be a sailor," said Floki, a little chagrined at the inference to being tired. "When do I leave?"

"As soon as you can choose your crew and get the supplies aboard," said Steinn. "If you pass through to the west, sail only a few days to the south, that is, if there is a way to the south. I would not want you to get ice bound in a strange land. I don't have to tell you that winter comes early at this latitude, and you will be sailing even farther to the north. Be sure to take plenty of warm clothing with you. If you are successful in finding a passage, we will decide when you return whether to settle at your island in the great lake or continue our search for the land of the bison."

"I will take the same eleven men that were with me before. They are good sailors, and we get along well," said Floki, as the meeting broke up. Steinn was amazed that he and Floki had done all the talking. The other men must be waiting to see which way the wind blew before taking sides. He would just have to make sure that the wind blew in his favor.

III

Time passed slowly for Steinn as he patiently awaited the return of the explorers. His father and grandfather before him had longed to sail to this new land in search of the grassy plains, but neither of them could raise the funds to finance such a voyage. If the crisis had not arisen in Greenland, forcing him to make a decision, he, too, would probably never have sailed. But now that he had come this far, he wanted more than anything to find the land of the bison. His people, for that is how he now thought of them, could flourish in such a land

While others brought timbers from Markland, only a short distance across the strait, to build two new ships, Steinn's first project was to rebuild the ancient blacksmith forge and charcoal kiln across the brook from the ruins of the ancient village. The green wood left over from the shipbuilding would make the best charcoal, but that wood was needed at the new drying kiln. Ships couldn't be made from uncured lumber. Steinn gathered the less desirable driftwood along the beach to make the fuel he needed to smelt iron. He passed the days by heating and shaping nails into arrow points; mending sails and rigging on the two older ships; sharpening axes and swords; and anything else to keep busy, but still the days dragged by. He even tried his hand at smelting the nodules of bog iron left behind by the builders of the smithy. Only one fifth of the iron could be recovered from the nodules and that was filled with impurities. The metal had to be heated and hammered, folded and hammered again, repeatedly, until the slag was finally beaten out. He became quite adept at making arrow and spear points from the bog iron, but he was nowhere close to being good enough to make a knife or axe. That task would require more skill at tempering the metal than he possessed.

After a month passed, he began to worry that maybe the exploration should have been postponed until next spring, even though that would have delayed leaving this place a whole year. He would never forgive himself if Floki and the other men were lost to winter storms or became ice bound—an ever-present danger in these northern latitudes. There weren't enough supplies on board the ship to see the men through the winter, and every day that passed brought cold weather a little closer.

Finally, after fifty days of tense waiting, a shout rang out on the seashore! A sail had been sighted to the north. When Steinn ran down to the beach, the sail was nothing more than a tiny white square on the horizon. Whoever had first seen the small white speck truly had perfect vision. Steinn was so filled with excitement and relief that he could hardly contain himself. When after half an hour the ship reached shore, he was the first one into the cold water to help beach the vessel.

After hearty greetings with much backpounding, the crew was allowed to eat or sleep as each saw fit, but tonight there would be a homecoming feast, and the squawberry wine would flow freely. Steinn could hardly wait to hear the results of the voyage. So far, he had been told absolutely nothing. What if no passage had been found? Would he be able to accept defeat and put the grassy plains out of his mind? There was no need to torture himself with such thoughts. If he would just be patient, the results of the voyage would be revealed in due time.

Since no lodge was large enough for all the people at one time, the feasting took place outside. The air was nippy after the sun went down, but two huge bonfires helped keep the cold at bay and provided light. A temporary table, now heavily laden with food, had been set up between the fires. There were no benches, but logs had been placed at a distance from the fires to accommodate those that wanted to sit. The sailors were served first and given the choicest morsels of food. Steinn wanted Floki free to talk as soon as possible.

Steinn was too anxious to be very hungry, and just when he thought that he could wait no longer, Floki rubbed his stomach and let go a great belch. "That was a feast fit for a king," he said, a little groggy from the wine. "If that was our only reward for making the voyage, it would be enough. But I have good news for you, Steinn. We did indeed find a westward passage. Sixteen days voyage to the north and west, after rounding a rocky cape, we were, indeed, able to sail to the south. Taking your advice not to go too far, we sailed for another eight days before reluctantly turning back. No one knows how much farther we could have gone. This seems to be a land without limits, and I am anxious to see more of it. Next spring, I must admit, we just might find your land of grass. We saw such a great herd of migrating caribou along one shore that I now concede that the story about the great herds of bison is quite possible. We had fresh meat aplenty."

Steinn could hardly contain his excitement! Moreover, to have Floki in agreement with him was much more than he had expected. Now would come the hard part: waiting until they could safely set out on what he hoped would be their final voyage.

The long winter days seemed to drag by. There was not much one could do outside during the winter, but when the weather permitted the men would go hunting for moose and caribou, even though there was enough meat to see them through the winter. The hunting helped break the monotony. People living in such close quarters tended to get edgy. On the outings, Steinn would not permit fewer than ten men in a party to venture away from the village for fear that the natives might attack. Until now all contact with them had been on a friendly basis, but one could never be too cautious.

When the first signs of spring finally appeared, Steinn began thinking about the food that would be needed to sustain his people on the voyage to the grassy plains. There was little doubt in his mind, now, that such a place existed. He hadn't read the whole document to the people, but if he saw the landmarks described in it, he was sure that he would recognize them. He didn't want to reveal everything in the document until some part of it was confirmed.

The Norge couldn't spare the time after the weather began to warm to gather enough food supplies for the coming voyage, so Steinn decided to see what could be bought from the natives. The number of salmon in the brook had been depleted over the winter months. With many of the men out hunting and fishing, Steinn gathered a small party for a trading expedition. With a bag full of iron arrow points, a few small knives, spools of string that he was sure the native women would like, and a bag of pretty but cheap glass beads and trinkets, the party set sail for the nearest native village.

After nearly a full day of sailing to the south, they put in at a narrow-protected cove at the southern end of a large bay. The cove was surrounded by low, forested hills that afforded some protection from harsh winter winds, a very good location for a village. Some of the native hunters had seen the Norge ships before, at a distance, and they were very much in awe of the large vessels. Being unsure of the intentions of the hairy, light skinned men in such strange clothing, the natives would not at first venture down to the beach. Then after Steinn stepped ashore alone and unarmed, a few of the native men, carrying bows and spears, cautiously approached. When Steinn spread a moose skin on the sand and spread his trade goods out upon it, more of the natives approached. Soon, every man, woman, and child in the village had turned out, with the smaller children peering cautiously from behind their mother's legs.

Every exposed area of the native's skin was painted red, making them look almost inhuman to the Norge. Redmen became the common name for them from that day.

The men in the ship were cautioned to make no overt move unless the natives became belligerent, but they were to keep weapons handy just in case. This precaution was unnecessary, as the natives were interested only in the trade goods.

Steinn chose a small piece of driftwood lying nearby and demonstrated how easily one of the knives he had made would cut the wood, curling up one shaving after another with apparent ease. A murmur of awe went through the men in the crowd. Such a thing was impossible with stone tools, and they had no knowledge of metals, other than a few pieces of copper, which was much too soft to hold such a keen edge. Most of the women had eyes only for the beads and string--the men for the knives and arrowheads. For his next demonstration, Steinn asked one of the men aboard the ship to hand him an arrow. Showing the native men what an arrow looked like with an iron point, he signed that he would like to use one of their bows. Taking aim at a beached log thirty yards away, he shot the arrow into it. Recovering the arrow, he showed the native men that the arrowhead was undamaged; whereas, a stone point would probably have been shattered. The arrow was passed from one to another, each one nodding sagely before handing it to the next man.

A bead and a spool of string were passed around among the women. They had never before seen such a slender thread as this, and so strong. A much better seam could be sewn with such a string, much better than with rawhide. After the items were passed around, Steinn got down to the business of trading. Through signs and pictures drawn in the sand, he was able to make himself understood. After the price of dried caribou, moose, bear, or fish was established, Steinn made the natives understand that he would be back in two months to do the actual trading. He required that the meat and fish be dried but allowed the natives to keep the animal hides for themselves. The Norge already had enough warm clothing made of wool. The skins would just be in the way on the voyage to their new home.

After a leisurely voyage home, netting a few fish on the way, Steinn spent the days of waiting making more knives, since that was what the native men seemed to want most. He was afraid that there would not be enough trade goods to go around. To make a knife, two large nails were heated until they were white hot and then hammered together until they were welded into a single unit. After being heated again, the metal was beaten to a uniform thickness to make a blade. A third nail was then welded to the rear of the blade, on which was mounted a wooden handle. The blade was then shaped to a point, and lastly it was sharpened. He could manufacture only two knives per day, which would put close to sixty more knives into the trade. There would not be enough knives to satisfy everyone he was sure, but he hoped that there would be no trouble from the natives who came up short.

The second morning of knife making brought a curious young man, about twenty years of age and with a million questions, to watch Steinn work. His name was Rolf Arnarson. He was probably the homeliest human being that Steinn had ever seen. His face was as flat as a shovel and his beard grew only in patches. His arms were too long, his legs were too short, but he was as strong as an ox. At first, Steinn considered him a curse, but then he realized that the youngster had a sincere desire to learn. During the third day, Steinn found that he actually enjoying the role of teacher, though with his limited knowledge of metalworking, he could have used a teacher himself.

Every day, after the fourth day, Rolf would work on into the evening, using the knowledge learned during the day to make a knife or arrowhead of his own. The finished product was so pathetic that Steinn would have laughed if the young man hadn't been so sincere in his effort to do well. The arrowheads he made were useable, but the knives were hardly worthy of the name. The blades were never the same thickness throughout, nor were they shaped or sharpened properly. By the time the two months were up, Steinn had grown quite fond of his inept pupil.

Rolf had buried his aging parents in Greenland only the year before, which was probably a godsend, as they would probably not have survived the voyage to Vinland. He was now living with his sister, Vigdis, and her husband, Gardar. Rolf didn't like Gardar at all. His brother-in-law was a lazy man and expected Vigdis to be his servant. Gardar had tried at first to assume an air of superiority with Rolf, but he discovered soon enough that Rolf was no man's servant. Something would have to change; the present relationship between them could not continue, Rolf decided.

The dawn of the sixtieth day found the trading party already under sail. Steinn wanted to be done with the trading and well on the way home before sundown. The natives had been friendly at the first meeting, but Steinn had no desire to spend the night near their village—they may try to take what they couldn't trade for. The day was sunny and cool with a steady ten-knot wind driving them swiftly southward. They made better time than on the first trip and beached the craft in the early afternoon. The natives were waiting expectantly beside neat piles of dried meat set out on caribou skins.

There was nowhere near the amount of meat that Steinn had expected. So much for his fear of coming up short on trade goods. The natives seemed downcast as they tried to apologize for the lack of game found. Hunting had been bad, as the herds of caribou had migrated far to the interior of the island. Some of the hunters didn't have enough meat to buy an arrowhead, much less a knife. What was lacking in meat was compensated for in fish. Steinn wound up giving his goods for far less meat than agreed upon. The natives were very grateful for the concession.

One middle aged man with a very noticeable limp, obviously unable to hunt, but badly wanting a knife, led a girl of about fourteen years by the elbow and placed her before Steinn. The poor creature stood with her head hanging in dejection, never once looking up. Through signs and gestures intermingled with words that Steinn did not understand, the man made it plain that he was willing to trade the girl for a knife for himself and a handful of beads for his wife. With his leg in such bad shape, he could hardly provide for his family. One less mouth to feed would be a blessing to him. The men on board, hooting and laughing, urged Steinn to go through with the trade, saying that the Norge men without wives would make good use of the girl.

Steinn almost exploded with pent-up rage. His jaw muscles bulged, and his face became almost as red as the painted natives. "This girl is not a whore and certainly not an animal," he said through clenched teeth. "The next man that makes a derogatory remark about her will feel my skinning knife in his guts. We have the name of being Christians, not savages. Some of you call these people savages. Well, take a good look at yourselves. Savage or no, she is still a human being. I will not have us stooping to the level of animals. I, too, have no wife, but what you men suggest makes me sick. Now, some of you come ashore and get this meat and fish aboard; there is no reason for us to tarry any longer.

"Steinn," said Rolf, timidly. "I would like to bargain with that man, if you will allow it. I would like to take the girl with me…as my wife." The chins of some of the men dropped at these words, but they dared not say anything. They had no desire to see if Steinn had made an idle threat.

"Are you serious Rolf? I won't have this girl treated badly," said Steinn, with anger still in his voice.

"Yes, sir, I am totally serious. With my looks, I know that none of our own girls will ever give me a second thought. I would like to be married. It is time that I made a break with my sister and her husband. I think that I am old enough and mature enough to be a husband. I will be good to her, Steinn; this I solemnly promise. We can have the marriage ceremony and baptism as soon as we return home, to our own village."

"No, we will have the marriage ceremony right here before the girl's parents, that is, if they accept your offer. That way, they can be assured that their daughter will have a husband and be treated with dignity, not as communal property," he said, as he looked at the crew. "Go ahead then, see what you can do. We will have another ceremony tomorrow."

Rolf jumped down to the beach with a grin that split his face in half. Holding his knives and points out before the father, he gestured at the girl. The man took a knife from Rolf's hand and examined it closely. Although the knife was superior to any blade that he had ever owned, he could readily see that the workmanship was inferior to the knives that Steinn had made. With a look of regret, he shook his head no, put the knife back in Rolf's hand, took the arrowheads, and pointed at Steinn's knives. "Well, I guess my knife isn't good enough for him," said Rolf, dejectedly.

Steinn handed the man one of his own knives, as well as a handful of beads and a spool of thread. The man's face beamed with joy as he nodded his agreement. This was a much better deal than he had expected. He gave the beads and thread to his wife. The girl, who had spent the whole time holding onto her mother's arm, had never raised her eyes from the ground. Her mother hugged her, said something to her, and then urged her toward Rolf. The girl, with tears coursing down her cheeks, meekly obeyed.

"I'll pay you for the knife and beads, Steinn," said Rolf. "Somehow."

"Forget it, Rolf. Consider them a wedding present," said Steinn.

Steinn had no idea what kind of marriage ceremony the natives went through, but he thought a simple demonstration would suffice. Taking a piece of string, he tied the girl's right little finger to Rolf's left little finger and had them hold their hands up for all to see. "I now pronounce you man and wife," he said in a voice loud enough for all to hear. "I want you to know, Rolf, that this may be an unorthodox ceremony, but I consider it a binding contract. Do you agree?" he said more quietly.

"Yes, sir, I sure do. This girl is now my lawful wife, and I am going to call her Helga, in honor of my mother."

"So be it. Let's go home," Steinn said.

"Uh, Steinn, what about the string?"

Steinn laughed. "You can remove it; it's served its purpose."

With adoring eyes, Rolf looked at his wife and gently lifted her aboard. As they were about to cast off, Helga's mother came running down to the beach with a small bundle that contained all of the girl's worldly possessions. Rolf caught the bundle in one huge hand and handed it to Helga. As the native village receded from view, she hugged the bundle to her breast as if her life depended on it. Steinn wondered what thoughts and fears were coursing through the poor girl's mind at this moment. He would have been surprised to know that she considered this band of pale-skinned, bearded men the ugliest creatures that she had ever seen, and hardly fit to be called human. And the odor that emanated from their bodies was almost nauseating to her. Mothers of the Beothuk tribe had for generations entertained their children with tales of pale, bearded bogeymen who had once lived on the northern end of the island. The girl had never dreamed that such tales were based on fact.

The voyage home took much longer, since the wind was uncooperative. The only happy person on board seemed to be Rolf. He held his wife's left hand and talked to her incessantly. She sat clutching her meager possessions with her right hand and staring unblinkingly at the bottom of the boat. Steinn fervently hoped that the poor girl would eventually make the adjustment to Norge society.

The sun was coming up as they moored the ship in the shallow bay. After a few hours sleep, Steinn was ready to distribute the meat and fish among the other ships and begin packing for the voyage ahead. It was now the first week of June and most of the ice should be broken up in the northern seas. Once they rounded the northernmost point and turned toward the south, the weather should improve markedly as the summer progressed. Merely thinking about the new lands made Steinn's heart race. Even though he had never lived in the land of the bison, he had a feeling akin to nostalgia every time he thought about it.

The new ships were launched and outfitted with time to spare. The shipbuilders were proud of their handiwork and several of them wanted to be the new captains, requiring Steinn to choose the ones he considered the most capable. Resentment arose among the rejected men, but there was no help for it. They would get over their hurt feelings in time. There was no way possible to please everybody.

The provisions were equally divided among the five ships, but not much else was accomplished that afternoon, as the people seemed to be dragging their feet. If he didn't get them away from this place soon, Steinn reasoned, some of the less venturesome souls wouldn't want to leave at all. It had been his heart's desire to find the fabled grasslands from the moment as a youth that he had first read the ancient document, and nothing was going to make him give up the quest after coming this far.

Steinn was up before dawn the next morning to supervise the final loading of the ships. By continually haranguing the people, he was able to complete the task by mid-morning. He selected one person from each dwelling to make a thorough final survey of the village to make sure nothing valuable was being left behind. With everyone finally on board, the ships were launched, with Floki in the lead and Steinn bringing up the rear. If an emergency arose, he wanted to be in the best position to come to the aid of the other ships.

Some of the women set up a wail just as they had when they had left Greenland. Steinn, too, felt a twinge of nostalgia as he turned to look at the meadow that had been his home for the past few months. No doubt, they could have thrived on the island as long as peace with the redmen was maintained, but this place would never have replaced the image of the land of the bison that haunted his mind.

It was always exciting to be headed for a new land, but too, there was always that feeling of apprehension that accompanied venturing into the unknown. Hopefully, they would be in their new and permanent homeland long before cold weather began. There wouldn't be enough time to search out the best location for a new village, build substantial dwellings, and lay in the winter's supply of meat if the voyage was a long one. The best that they could hope for, as on the island of Vinland, would be temporary shelters and enough food to see them through the winter.

On the fourth day of sailing, they left the forested shores of Markland behind. They were now north of the tree line, with only stunted willows and patches of grass giving the land a tint of green. Until they turned south once again, there would be nothing but a bleak rocky coastline with deep narrow inlets to break the horizon. The temperature became noticeably colder with each day's progress to the northwest, and when on the ninth day the coastline turned sharply southward, Steinn dared think that they had made exceptionally good time. However, his hopes were dashed when Floki allowed him to catch up. As the ships came abreast, Floki explained that there was a huge bay to the left and that they could save a whole day of sailing by cutting straight across the mouth.

"Thank you for explaining. I would have been wondering why we had left the coastline. You have been this way before; you know what you are doing. Sail on," said Steinn.

Before they had completed the crossing of the bay, the wind had increased dramatically. By the time land was sighted again, the sky was overcast and a light, almost freezing, rain was falling. Floki, seeking shelter, guided the ships dangerously close to the shore. Luckily, a protected bay dotted with small islands lay just ahead. At least there, they hoped, would be shelter from the wind and rain.

Lady luck was smiling upon them. At the very back of the bay was a line of cliffs, with a narrow strip of sandy beach between the cliffs and the sea. There was a high concave depression in one cliff, the top of which actually overhung the beach. It wasn't a cave by any means, but it afforded the only shelter that was available.

While the women brought food from the ships, the men and boys dragged driftwood to the campsite. With two large fires, one on either side of the camp, radiating much heat, the light rain blown under the overhang was evaporated as fast as it fell. That night the people, wrapped in furs and huddled close together between the two fires, slept reasonably well.

The morning dawned bright and cold. The wind was brisk, and the temperature had dropped several degrees, but the seas were not so high as to prevent sailing. They were soon under way once more and, thanks to the wind, made very good time. The time saved by crossing the mouth of the large bay was practically negated by the holdover during the storm, but the brisk wind, which was driving the ships faster than yesterday, was helping to make up the loss.

Around noon of the fifteenth day, they reached the northernmost point of the voyage, rounded a rocky cape, and headed south again. A cheer went up and spirits were raised visibly. The wind blowing out of the south slowed their progress, as that was the very direction they needed to sail. It was necessary to tack in a southwesterly direction for a time, away from the coastline, and then tack to the southeast until the coastline was sighted once again. This pattern had to be repeated every few hours, slowing their progress drastically. Spirits remained high, however, as each day that passed brought them closer to their final destination. When trees were sighted again, many of the men wanted to take a day and go hunting, but Steinn wanted to sail on. He refused to relax until the large river mentioned in the document which entered the sea from the southwest was found.

The only gloomy person on board was Helga. Nothing had changed as far as she was concerned. She was among strangers, in a strange environment, and headed for a strange new land. Even her husband was a stranger to her. Though he talked to her almost constantly, she had never understood the first word, and had no interest in learning. Yet, he was the only familiar thing aboard the ship, other than the bundle in her lap, and she would not permit Rolf to get more than a few feet from her—not even to relieve himself behind the curtain at the rear of the ship.

The ancient narrative told of a large river that entered the sea from the southwest, but just how large was anybody's guess. How Steinn wished for a map. Even descriptions that were less ambiguous would be a big help. After eleven days of sailing toward the south with the shoreline always on the port side, they came to the southernmost point of the sea. For the last few days, the sea had been dotted with islands, large and small, making night sailing hazardous, to say the least. The few remaining ice floes were white and much easier to see. No time had been wasted exploring while on the southward journey, since all the rivers encountered thus far were small and flowed from the east. Now that they had reached the southern most point and the coastline had turned to the northwest, every large river entering the sea would have to be thoroughly investigated.

Only hours after turning the ships northwest, the first river was found, and flowing from exactly the right direction. Steinn, with a small boat made especially for this purpose and a crew of six men, rowed up the swift channel, leaving the remaining men to fish, hunt, and forage for anything edible. Fifteen leagues from its mouth, the river split. According to the ancient document this could not be the right river. The boat was allowed to drift with the current back to the mouth of the river. The other ships had netted a few fish, and a small basket was filled with dried berries that were still clinging to the bushes. If something substantial did not turn up soon, the remaining food would have to be rationed.

Another day's journey put them at the mouth of another river, but the channel of this one was divided by an island. No island was mentioned in the document. They sailed on. Dawn found them between a large stream on the left and a large island to the right. This one did not fit the description either. For two days they sailed to the north, then the coastline led them in a westerly direction for a day and a half, before another substantial stream was encountered. At the mouth of this one, were numerous small islands. This was not the river they were searching for, but on the nearest of the islands could be seen a huge white bear feasting on the remains of a caribou that had probably drowned crossing the river and had washed up on the beach. The bear was difficult to distinguish against the patches of snow in the background, but the snow, still unmelted on the northern slopes and in the shade of evergreen trees, was tinted pink all around the caribou carcass. The bloody snow stood out like a red flag.

Steinn led the ships in a wide arc to the backside of the island so as not to disturb the feasting bear, before having the other ships anchor in the river channel. He beached his own ship and asked for five volunteers to go with him to take the bear. Nearly every man on board who owned a weapon--whether bow, axe, or spear--eagerly grabbed it and stepped forward. Steinn had to choose the men himself. It was a difficult task, as he didn't want to offend anyone. He chose young, strong men, for fear that older men may not be agile enough to avoid the bear if it attacked. The first man chosen was Rolf—big, strong, and quick. He grabbed a heavy spear and jumped to the beach. The other four men chose bows and arrows, while Steinn chose a heavy broadax.

When the men were out of sight, Helga, unnoticed by the others on the ship, tied a rope to the prow of the ship and quietly let herself down to the beach. Running as fast as her short legs would carry her, she soon caught sight if the hunters. She followed at a discrete distance, using the available cover to mask her movements. When Steinn motioned the hunters to stop, she knelt behind a bush, hardly daring to breathe. She could see the great white bear, as the men stealthily approached it from down wind. As quietly as a mouse she crept on hands and knees to within twenty yards of the men. Carefully and soundlessly, she crawled under a tangle of low bushes and watched as the men slowly approached the feasting bear. With their attention riveted

on the big bruin, the hunters never suspected that she was anywhere around.

Suddenly, the bear came to its feet to better position the carcass. The hunters froze in their tracks, being only ten yards from
their prey. The nearsighted bear, engrossed in the act of gorging
itself, suspected nothing. When the bear put its whole head inside
the belly cavity of the carcass, Steinn motioned the men to make
a line, with himself at one end and Rolf at the other. The four
archers, with arrows nocked, waited for a signal.

When Steinn gave the signal, four feathered shafts seemed to
sprout simultaneously behind the bear's right shoulder. The bear
roared and jerked its head around with such force that it lost its balance and toppled over on its left side. The beast regained its feet and
went around in a circle biting at the shafts protruding from its ribs.
Then the great bruin, with bloody froth blowing from its nostrils,
noticed the line of men. With an angry snarl, it stood up on its hind
legs, and four more arrows appeared in its throat and chest. Though
mortally wounded, the great animal was still very dangerous.

The bear launched itself at the man nearest Rolf. Already getting weak from the eight arrow wounds, it made a slow lumber-
ing charge. They all stood their ground, until stein yelled for the
archers to step back. Maybe they could have out run the bear, but
no one wanted to have the wounded animal coming at him from
behind. Rolf, with his heavy spear held waist high with both hands,
stepped between the man to his left and the bear. As the bear
raised its forequarters to knock Rolf to the ground, he plunged
the spear deep into the bruin's chest cavity. Releasing the spear
shaft, Rolf immediately threw himself to the side, away from the
collapsing bear, but the animal fell dead across his legs, pinning
him to the ground.

Thinking that Rolf was in mortal danger, Helga burst forth from her hiding place, and screaming like a banshee, launched herself atop the bear. One of the panicky bowmen almost released an arrow at what he thought was another animal attacking. "Helga! What are…? Get this beast off me!" Rolf roared.

All the other men working together were able to roll the bear far enough so that Rolf could free his feet.

Heart pounding, he stood up. When he made a step to see if anything was broken, his feet slipped on the frozen snow. His boots were slippery from the animal's blood. He hit the ice hard and slid on his back, legs pointed at the sky, down a twenty-foot slope. Everyone, including Helga, had a hearty laugh, and when Rolf tried to stand again, he took another spill, starting a new gale of laughter from the spectators.

Helga was laughing mostly from relief that Rolf was not hurt. In a flash, she had come to realize that this man was her life; he was her only refuge in a world of strangers. When she had seen him go down under the huge animal, her only thought was to divert the bear's attention so that he could escape. Now that she could see he was safe, she was giddy with relief.

Rolf, not wanting to slip again, came crawling up the slope on hands and knees. Helga touched Steinn's arm to get his attention. Pointing at the bear, she asked in Beothuk, her native language: "What is your word for this animal?" Steinn, not understanding, gave her a puzzled look. She tried again, only this time she shrugged as she asked the question.

"Oh, that's a bear," Steinn said in the Norse tongue. "Bear," he repeated.

Helga pointed at Rolf crawling up the slope. "Bear," she said, with a giggle.

"Yes, I do believe you are right," Steinn said with a chuckle.

Rolf was afraid to try to stand again until he was off the ice. As silly as he knew he must look, he continued to crawl until he had attained bare ground. After wiping the blood from his boots with a handful of leaves and loose snow, he stood up. Baring his teeth and arms outstretched, he started toward Helga growling deep in his throat. "Laugh at your husband, will you?" he growled. Helga shrieked with mock terror and turned to run, but Rolf grabbed her around the waist. Carrying her in his arms as easily as a child, Rolf deposited her in a nearby snowdrift and scooped snow down her collar. She shrieked with laughter as she rubbed a handful of snow in his face. The laughter faded as a tender look came into Rolf's eyes. He kissed her forehead and whispered: "I love you, Helga." She didn't understand the words, but she understood the look. He helped Helga to stand, and they walked to where the others had begun skinning the bear.

"That is quite a woman you've got there, Rolf," said Steinn, as he smiled at Helga. "But you need to teach her to stay out of harms way from now on. That was really something, though, the way she attacked that bear with nothing but teeth and nails," he chuckled. "Why don't you two go and tell the others to bring the ships around?"

"She really is something, isn't she? She has been so withdrawn ever since we left her village that I was worried about her, but something seems to have changed suddenly. I think I'm going to like it."

"I noticed the change myself. I've also noticed the patience that you've had with her. You're a good man, Rolf. Now, go get the others."

As they began the short trek to the far side of the island, Helga took Rolf's hand and smiled up at him. When they reached the ships, Rolf gave a brief account of the kill to the people on board, then told them to weigh anchor, as he and Helga would walk back across the island. This time it took them more than an hour to make the short trip back.

Everyone had his fill of bear meat, and there was enough meat left for another day. With everyone sated, the voyage was continued. The fifth river encountered also had a large island at its confluence with the sea. They sailed for two more days and were again in need of meat when they came to the largest river yet seen. Steinn was so positive that this was the right stream that all the ships were included in the exploration. They sailed as far as possible up the long estuary, then sails were furled, and they began to row. After two days of continuous rowing, with two teams relieving each other every hour, they came to a series of rapids in the river. Now, there was no doubt at all in Steinn's mind that they were on the right track. This stretch of shoals was another of the landmarks mentioned in the chronicle. Steinn was jubilant.

It was quite a struggle to get the ships past the rapids, but by using ropes to pull with and long poles to push with, the task was finally accomplished. The men who had braved the icy water were the most relieved when the last ship was brought through. The river, above the shoals, widened into a large lake. On the southern shore of the lake, a temporary camp was hastily made. They were again in forested terrain where plenty of firewood was available. A large fire was built so that the ones who had gotten wet could get warm, and their clothes could be dried.

IV

Helga, from the day of the bear kill, was a completely different person. She began to have an interest in everything that took place around the camp. The women that were friends of Vigdis, Rolf's sister, tried to include Helga in their daily activities, as much as the language barrier would permit. Her eagerness to learn helped the women to accept her so much the faster. Having Helga as a student gave them something to break the tediousness of the voyage.

There were those, of course, that still resented the presence of a Skraeling in their midst, but they knew better than to make an issue of the matter. Not only would they have to withstand Steinn's anger, but also Rolf--whose temper was quick to flare--was very protective of his young wife. There were some who would rather face Steinn than Rolf. Steinn, as leader of the Norge, had to consider the far-ranging effects of his actions--Rolf had no such responsibility.

Rolf built a lean-to of poles and spruce limbs and spread his bedding underneath. Helga settled into the role of being a wife and appeared to thrive on the activity. She appeared to miss her former life not at all any more. Rolf adored his bride and watched her every move; he couldn't possibly have been more contented.

Since he was sure that they were now on the right track to the land of tall grass, Steinn was no longer overly concerned about time. If they didn't reach the land of the bison this year, they were sure to attain their goal the next. Several groups of men went hunting, while others plied the lake for fish. For three days, the men brought in a variety of animals and fish—enough to last another week.

Helga began the initial process of tanning three deer hides by scraping the fat and flesh from them and pegging them down in the sun to dry.

The fourth morning was warm and beautiful as they resumed the voyage. They soon entered a series of lakes, dotted with islands and with bays and inlets so numerous that following the course of the river was most difficult. Many times, they were forced to backtrack, making progress upstream very slow indeed. It required four days to accomplish what should have been a three-day journey. But when on the fourth day they entered the largest lake that any of them, except for Floki and his crew, had ever seen, Steinn knew for certain that this was the grand lake mentioned in the ancient document. It was as big as an inland sea, and the water, which was fresh, was teeming with pike, pickerel, and white fish. Steinn was tempted to search out a site to settle, but the lure of the great bison herds, and an ever-abundant supply of meat, drew him on.

Steinn knew that they had to be nearing their final destination, but there wouldn't be enough warm weather left to explore the land, build a permanent village, and lay aside enough provisions for the coming winter. Sailing to the southern end of the great lake took another three days, while another day was spent looking for a good location for a winter camp. They found a long narrow peninsula that jutted far out into the lake. There the camp would be more exposed to the elements than somewhere in a secluded cove, but the site would be more easily defended, as an attack by land could come from only one direction.

After all the sailing that summer, they were at the same latitude as they had been in Vinland where they had spent the previous winter. Again, as on the island, everyone available worked hard to build shelters that would withstand the winter wind and snow. The trees in this area were much larger than those on the island, making the lodge building much faster and easier. While the women and larger children and some of the men were building shelters, the best hunters and fishermen were busy laying in a supply of food. The forest was home to an abundance of moose and deer, and there were times when the nets almost burst from the great number of white fish caught. It would be very difficult, Steinn believed, to get the people to leave this site next spring.

Steinn busied himself with hammer and chisel making triangular mooring holes in three large boulders along the shore. Once the holes were finished, the ships could be easily moored by simply dropping a rope and a peg into the hole. Fishermen had recently found such holes at other sites around the lake, convincing Steinn that others of his race had at one time lived on this lake. When he overheard the captain of one of the ships mention a river, red with sediment, entering the lake from the south, his conviction was overwhelming that they were close to their final destination. The red river was the last of the landmarks mentioned in the ancient document.

The men continued to hunt and fish every day, weather permitting, to keep the food supply from dwindling. The lake was sure to partially freeze over as winter progressed--if not out in the deepest part, at least along the shoreline--making sailing impossible.

As their stay lengthened, the animals within easy walking distance of the camp had quickly learned to be wary of the hunters, making it necessary to go farther from camp to hunt. They soon began to sail to some predetermined location on the lake, go hunting, load the harvest on the ship, and sail back home, never having to tire themselves out by walking great distances.

One cold sunny morning Floki's ship came sailing back to camp hours before it was expected. As usual when hunters returned several men from the camp converged on the shore to help with the unloading. Steinn, his curiosity aroused by the early arrival, which usually meant trouble, strolled slowly toward the ship. He sensed that something was amiss even before he could hear what was being said. Floki and his crew, in a jovial manner, were relating the morning's adventure as they tossed bundles of meat wrapped in fresh skins to the men on shore.

"You should have seen those mangy curs run," said Floki, laughing heartily. "They probably won't stop until they can hide behind their wives' skirts. The men on shore, knowing that Steinn was approaching, wanted to join in the laughter, but they were afraid of the consequences.

"What is so humorous?" asked Steinn. He knew that the hunters usually brought back whole carcasses, not skins laden with meat.

"Oh, nothing much," said Floki. "We're just happy because we had such an easy hunt this morning. Right men? The meat was practically given to us," he added, causing his crew to chuckle.

"Why don't you tell me the whole story? I like a good laugh now and then. That is, if something is actually funny." The tone of Steinn's voice hinted that he wouldn't be amused.

"Four of my crew and I were stealthily making our way along a game trail when we met face to face nearly a dozen Skraelings loaded down with bundles of meat. Well, I guess they had never seen such hairy two-legged creatures as us before. They yelped like kicked dogs, dropped their bundles, and took off like foxes with their tails were on fire. Of course, we yelled a little to urge them on. Then, we simply reversed our course and carried the meat back to the ship, and there it is. Like I said, the easiest hunt I've ever been on," said Floki, with a jocular air.

Steinn, with all seriousness, thought for a few seconds before speaking. He didn't want to alienate Floki and his crew any more than they already were, but for safety's sake, the natives shouldn't be antagonized either. It would be months before they would be able to move on; he couldn't take the chance of provoking the natives to take revenge.

"Floki, I know you didn't see any harm in taking the meat but look at it from the native's viewpoint. No one was attacked; no body got hurt; but it could possibly bring us trouble before we leave here next spring. We can't afford to make enemies if we intend to live in this new land. I think the meat should be returned to its rightful owners. They've probably already been back to look for it."

"My men and I are tired, we have no intention of going out again today," said Floki, with all humor gone from his voice.

"What seemed to be the native's destination?" asked Steinn.

"Probably the village at the stream across the lake northwest of here. At least that was the general direction in which they were headed."

"You men put those bundles aboard my ship," said Steinn to the men milling around on shore. He didn't like having to personally undo Floki's mistake, but he didn't know what else to do. If he pressed the issue, a fight would undoubtedly ensue. The time would come, Steinn felt sure, when Floki would challenge his leadership, especially if he could persuade a few more men to follow him. But until that time came, Steinn intended to do whatever was necessary to keep everyone together. If that meant bending over backward, then so be it.

"I'll need a small crew to help me manage the sail," he said, after the meat was aboard. "Any of you men want to volunteer?" Five men stepped forward. "Good. Get your bows and quivers just in case." Steinn would have liked to take Rolf along, but he was out with another hunting party. He had come to depend on the burly young man, and Rolf was always eager to lend a helping hand.

The ship was rowed a short distance from shore by the six men before the sail was hoisted. Steinn took the helm and set a northwesterly course, using a lodestone shaped like a fish to stay on course. When the western shoreline came into clear view, Steinn, alerted by the action of a school of minnows, ordered the sail furled to slow the ship and the fishnet cast astern. The net, when retrieved, held perhaps fifty whitefish. He hoped this small extra offering would appease the natives.

When they beached the ship, the village in all appearances, except for smoke coming from the lodges, seemed to have been abandoned. Steinn and two other men went ashore and the bundles of meat were tossed to them one at a time. A moose hide was laid on the beach beside the bundles, and the whitefish were stacked like cordwood on it. Steinn and the others climbed aboard, and as the ship was being rowed away from shore, several natives came out of the forest and began to cautiously make their way toward the beach. As the sail caught the wind, Steinn waved to the natives. They didn't wave back. Steinn hoped, as the village slowly slipped from sight, that his efforts had not been in vain.

For the next three days, Floki and his crew moped around camp, refusing to hunt, and avoiding nearly everyone, Steinn in particular. Floki's decision about keeping the meat had been over-turned, and like an errant child, his actions had been corrected. In Floki's opinion, he had lost face before the whole camp. Early the fourth morning he and his men loaded their ship with sup-plies, saying nothing to anyone, and sailed to the southeast. A river entered the grand lake from that direction, but it had not been explored. The ship never returned, and no one saw any sign of Floki and his men again.

Not many days later, the first hint of winter blew in with rain turning to snow. The days had become much shorter and the nights longer. After the wind settled down, the world was white and quiet as death. Hunting and fishing came to a halt as the cold increased. It snowed almost daily until the lake began to freeze over. Weather permitting, the children were allowed outside to frolic in the snow, but as winter deepened, there was very little activity in the village, except on the best of days.

No one had any reason to venture very far afield as the snow accumulated. Twice, footprints were discovered at the outskirts of the village—the first time, the trail of a single person--the other, more than one. The footprints of the leader making the second trail had been stepped in by those following, but it was impossible to determine how many. However, no contact was made with the natives as the days slowly dragged on.

Before the lake had frozen over, the ships had been hauled above the water line and turned on their sides to prevent ice damage. The only break in the frozen lake that could be seen from camp was a hole that had to be reopened each morning for the taking of fresh water.

One bright morning in March, Steinn went outside after the sun had been up for an hour or more. It was clear and crisp, and at this hour, the sun gave forth no warmth at all. Yet, he could sense a change in the air and knew that today the spring thaw would begin. There were still another few weeks of cold weather to tolerate, but soon the ice would begin to break up, and he would be on his way south. As he stood with eyes closed facing the cold sun, he could picture himself in the vast, green grassland, drawing a bow as a great bison came within range. The arrow sails straight and true, and the huge animal takes a few steps and crumples. Oh, he could hardly wait to leave this place. The land of his dreams, he was sure, was only a few hundred leagues away, and patience was not one of his virtues.

Rolf came crawling from the low entranceway of his shelter. He was wearing clothing the likes of which Steinn had never seen before. His body, from neck to toe, was covered in finely worked deerskin. The suit was formfitting and supple as woolen cloth. Along the undersides of the sleeves hung tassels of skin, and across the chest was a patchwork of porcupine quills, dyed various colors. If the tassels and quills served any purpose, Steinn didn't know what it was, but they surely looked pretty. A collar made from the skin of the great white bear, with cuffs to match, contrasted with the tan of the suit. He had never seen such beautiful handiwork before. Rolf would be the envy of every man in camp, and Helga would surely have a busy future teaching the other women her skills.

Rolf was aglow with pride in new clothes, while at the same time he was embarrassed at the attention he was getting from Steinn and others who were beginning to brave the morning cold. Steinn was honestly stunned as he tested the suppleness of the skins with his fingers. Admirers soon swamped Rolf, as Helga looked on before the shelter entrance, her heart swelling with pride from the attention her husband was getting. She had worked all winter on the skins, and now her skills had made Rolf the most handsomely dressed man in the village. Even the women who had been slow to accept Helga looked at her with newfound admiration.

Everyone knew that as the woolen clothes brought from Greenland wore out that animal skins would have to take their place. Leather was nothing new to the Norge, but the style and workmanship of Rolf's clothes were at the same time strange and beautiful. Some of the admirers decided not to wait until their woolen clothes wore out before trying this new style of clothing.

V

As the Ice on the lake finally began to melt, Steinn ordered the ships turned upright and made ready for launching. He was sure that the grassy plains were so near that little provisioning was made for the trip. The ships were sent out only once to net as many fish as possible for the voyage south. The fishermen discovered that the snow on the western shore of the lake was not as deep as at the winter camp. Since the Norge had never lived close to a large lake before, they knew nothing of lake-effect snow. They had chosen the worst site possible to spend the winter.

Getting the people to leave the present camp wasn't as much of a problem as Steinn had anticipated. No one seemed to be attached to this point of land. Steinn had to admit it was a rather bleak place with nothing but water to look at in three directions, but it had kept them safe through the winter. Now, it was time to move on.

Steinn called a meeting in the center of the camp where everyone could attend. His proposal was to lead an exploration party south to look for the land of small lakes to the east of the Muddy River and then return for the others. On the other hand, if the majority wanted, they could abandon the present campsite and take the chance of finding a more suitable place to spend the next winter farther south. A vote was taken, and the decision to abandon the present campsite forever was unanimous.

The ships were quickly launched and loaded and soon under way. The atmosphere this time was one of going home after a long absence. Steinn's optimism had spread throughout the camp and all the Norge seemed to sense that a new beginning was near. Everyone could feel that the end of the long journey was at hand. After two winters in this strange land, hopefully, they were about to settle down in a permanent home. Overall, this meant more to the women than to the men, since the men tended to be more the explorer and adventurer types.

At dusk they were at the mouth of the Muddy River, where a hasty camp was prepared. Shortly after dawn the ships entered the muddy stream. Sails were useless here, and rowing against the current was hard, strenuous work, as the river was full from spring rains and snowmelt farther south. With the whole summer before them, the colonists were in no great hurry. Sometime around noon each day, the ships were anchored in whatever protected area could be found and some of the men would go hunting and exploring, while others were content to rest. No sightings of bison were made, but there were dried droppings to be seen everywhere, especially on the western side of the river. The farther one traveled toward the west the more scattered the trees became, finally giving way to the open prairie, the home of the bison.

As the ships were rowed slowly upstream, a native village was passed, but no attempt at contact was made. The natives stood awe-struck, staring at the large, strange boats and even stranger looking people aboard. Several of the children ran along the bank in order to keep the ships in sight as long as possible. Steinn tried to imagine what was going through the minds of those people.

However, if others of his kind had been here before, maybe the ships weren't so strange after all, unless of course, the memory of the others was too far in the past.

On the tenth day of a journey that could have been made in three days of good sailing, Steinn saw his first bison. In a meadow beside a small, clear stream flowing from the east, grazed a half dozen of the shaggy beasts. Twenty archers, including Steinn, disembarked and surrounded the small herd, driving it slowly toward the triangle of land at the confluence of the two streams. Just as the animals began to cast about looking for an escape route, the archers released their arrows. None of the animals went down immediately, but only one, a great bull, had the courage and strength to attempt to break through the line of men. Another volley of arrows brought the huge animal to an abrupt halt. The sting of the arrows made the bull change his mind. His desire was to turn back toward his companions, but his legs wouldn't obey. He gave a great bellow and crumpled where he stood.

The charge of the great beast had given Steinn an adrenaline high. Now, he couldn't calm down. As he walked from one animal to the next, looking lovingly at the great beasts, he realized that his long-held dream of bending a bow against a bison had just been fulfilled. Surely, it was a sign from God. This was the place of his longing. Here, in this very meadow, was the place where his next home must be built. He would call a meeting later. Now, there was work to be done.

The ships were anchored in the smaller stream, and men and women alike began the skinning and butchering of the animals. Steinn wiped his skinning knife on the shoulder of the great bull and gave his place up to someone else. Firewood was already being gathered. Soon, there would be meat roasting.

There weren't enough animals for everyone to work at skinning, leaving many people with nothing to do but to stand and watch. As Steinn once more walked from carcass to carcass, he saw Helga, with blood dripping from her chin, standing beside a disemboweled cow. He quickened his step to go to her aid, thinking someone had hurt her. He was about to ask what had happened when Helga took a bite from the chunk of fresh, steaming liver in her right hand. Steinn's stomach lurched. He averted his eyes and took a faltering step backward, walking away quickly before he became sick.

The aroma of roasting meat soon replaced the nauseous feeling with pangs of hunger. Steinn chose a thin cut of meat from the back strap of a cow and wove a slender pointed stick through it. Before the meat was thoroughly cooked, hunger forced Steinn to take a bite. He had never tasted meat quite like this before. It had a full, rich flavor. He ate the rest of that piece as it was and reached for another to put on his roasting stick.

After everyone had eaten until sated, Steinn called a meeting to ask if the people wanted to build a village at this site or move on. The affirmation of the site was loud and long; not a single objection was raised. This location seemed to have everything needed—the meadow was large and almost level, there were plenty of trees nearby, the small river had clear water for drinking, and surely there would be more bison to hunt.

There having been no time to build any kind of shelter before nightfall, people slept wherever they could find a place near the fires that were kept burning throughout the night. Since the native village was not so far away, guards were posted a short distance from the camp. Early the next morning the ring of axes could be heard throughout the forest. Substantial dwellings were being built but not nearly as big as the early explorers had built in Vinland. Although, everyone wanted very badly to settle here permanently, few believed that it would be so; therefore, why build a large earth-covered dwelling now? If everything worked out, the lodges could be enlarged later.

As a safety measure, Steinn wanted a palisade built across the triangle of land between the two rivers, but this could wait until after the lodges were finished. He built his own lodge facing the place where he intended to put a gate in the palisade wall. If an attack was ever made from that direction, the gate would be the weakest point in the wall, and that was where he wanted to be. The logs would be made to extend into the two rivers at both ends of the wall so that an enemy would have to swim to enter the village that way, putting him at a disadvantage. He hoped to live in peace with the natives, but one could never be too cautious.

A trench two feet deep was dug from one river to the other and logs, pointed at the top, were placed side by side in the trench until the wall was completed. After the palisade was finished and a watchtower built, Steinn relaxed enough to go exploring a few leagues to the east. Except for a tributary flowing into the clear stream from the south, he found nothing of interest.

The next day Steinn began to dismantle his ship, plank by plank, sorting the boards into piles to use in the building of smaller fishing boats. He wanted this action to convey a message to the people that this would be his permanent home. From this day forward, there would be no thought of turning back. Short excursions by hunters into the country to the east had found it dotted with small lakes that were filled with fish, but no more bison were seen. The smaller boats would be easier to handle and would have a shallower draft, making navigation of the small streams feasible. Soon, the other ship owners were following Steinn's example. There would be enough boats to have one on each of several different lakes at the same time, making frequent portaging between the lakes unnecessary.

The days were getting longer and much warmer, giving the meadow a green tint from the new grass that had begun to grow. Unknown to the Norge, great herds of bison would follow the sprouting grass into the northern plains in the springtime, and as autumn began, a reverse migration would begin toward the south.

A returning hunting party that had crossed the red river brought the exciting news that a massive herd of animals, seemingly without end, was making its way slowly north a short distance to the west. Everyone wanted to see this spectacle, but it wouldn't be prudent to leave the village completely unprotected. Nearly half of the villagers were chosen to take part in this hunt, with the promise that the others would get to go next time.

Using the newly constructed boats, the hunting party was ferried across the Red River—the obvious choice for a name--taking the better part of an hour. When everyone was safely on the western shore, the leaders set a fast pace and in another hour the herd was sighted. Everyone climbed to the top of a low ridge to get a better view. Such a multitude of animals had never before been seen by any of the Norge! Their excitement was so electric in nature that it seemed the very air was charged! Some of the men wanted to rush down to the herd immediately and begin the harvest, but Steinn, telling them to take cover behind some low bushes, pointed to a group of natives far off to the right who were beginning to advance on the herd. Others wanted to attack the natives and run them away from the herd, but common sense prevailed. There were far more than enough animals in this one herd to feed everyone, Norge and native alike.

About two hundred yards from the herd, the native hunters stopped and began draping wolf skins, with snout and ears intact, over their heads and backs. Hunkering down as low as possible, they began a slow stalk of the herd. Instead of heading straight toward the herd, the hunters moved parallel with it, ever so slowly inching closer. The bison seemed to pay no attention to the supposed wolf pack. When only a few yards from the herd, the hunters began to loose arrows into chosen targets, mostly the younger cows it seemed. The animals that had been shot would run a short distance, but having no understanding of what was happening, would stay with the herd until they dropped.

Steinn was certain that there was a reason why the natives used this method to hunt the bison. It had been easy for the Norge to surround the bison at the rivers, but it would be impossible to separate a portion of this great herd. A man would be gored or trampled in seconds. If he could find a place where the bison came close to cover, maybe enough animals could be harvested to redeem this excursion.

As he scanned the terrain to the south for some kind of cover, he saw a pack of real wolves milling around close by the bison. He was amazed at how little attention the herd paid the wolves. Obviously, the bison were accustomed to the presence of these predators. Steinn reasoned that it would be just as difficult for the wolves to separate and bring down a member of the herd as it would be for a man to do the same. Why then were they attending the herd? To wait for an old or sick animal to fall behind? He wished he had the time to watch the wolves until they made a kill. Maybe he could learn something useful. He had already learned much in the few minutes of watching the native hunters. Now, it seemed, if he wanted to be a successful bison hunter, he would have to spend some time trapping wolves.

"Let's stay low and move farther to the south away from the native hunters," said Steinn. "Maybe we can figure out some strategy by which we can get closer to the herd."

"With that many animals in front of us, why can't we just run in close, release our arrows, and retreat?" asked Pall, one of the younger men in the group.

"My guess is that those huge bulls at the perimeter of the herd are there for a reason," added Steinn. "Men on foot would be hard put to outrun one of those beasts."

When they were a safe distance from the native hunters, Steinn called a halt. There was nothing but grass in any direction--nothing that would hide a man until he could get close enough to release an arrow. As an experiment, he hunkered down and approached the herd. Seeing the strange figure, one of the bulls disengaged himself from the herd to investigate. Steinn retreated and was about to give up on the prospect of taking an animal when the young man, Pall, who had spoken earlier, ran past him straight for the herd. Several of the older men ran a few steps after the youngster, yelling for him to stop.

When only a few feet from the herd Pall shot an arrow into the heart of a cow and turned without pause to begin a hasty retreat away from the herd. The bull that was curious about Steinn had seen the running figure, even before the arrow was released, and had already begun his charge. The other bowmen, almost out of range but desperate to help Pall, released a volley of arrows at the charging bull. Their aim was less than perfect, as there were arrows protruding from every part of the bull's body, from front to rear, but none seemed to have penetrated into a vital area.

As the bull neared his retreating quarry, he hooked the seat of Pall's pants with a thrust that came very close to impaling the youth on the right horn. Feeling resistance, the bull tossed his head backward, lifting Pall's feet clear of the ground and causing the seat of his pants to tear loose from the horn. The young man landed on his face--unhurt except for his dignity. The bull's momentum carried him past the boy by a few yards. As he came to a full stop in order to turn back and resume the charge, a dozen arrows found their mark. The huge animal took a few faltering steps and crumpled.

Just as Pall finished dusting himself off, Steinn grabbed the front of his shirt with both hands, lifting him off the ground. While shaking the boy like a rag doll, Steinn berated him unmercifully.

"I don't have to tell you how close you came to being killed, but I will tell you that if you ever do anything that stupid again, you will be banned from all hunting parties for the rest of your life. You didn't just endanger yourself; any one of us could have been gored to death by that monstrous animal. I'm going to charge this incident to your youth and inexperience, but you had better learn to think before you act if you expect to live long enough to become a man." Putting the young man down so hard on his feet that his knees buckled, Steinn added, "Let's see what we can do about getting these animals skinned. By the way, that was an excellent shot you made at the cow."

The youngster, almost in tears at the severe scolding, wanted to smile at the compliment, but his lips were trembling so badly the smile just wouldn't form. He hung his head to keep from meeting anyone's gaze and went to look for his bow.

The herd had veered away from the group of hunters, leaving the dead cow a safe distance away. The two animals were skinned and boned, with the meat piled on the skins. The hunting party had been so hastily and thoughtlessly assembled that no baskets or other containers had been brought in which to carry the meat back to camp. Four good-sized men could probably carry the meat of one animal tied inside a hide, but it was too bulky to be lifted unless slung from a pole. The nearest trees were some distance away toward the river. That would mean waiting until poles could be brought before the meat could be moved.

The only satisfactory solution was for every man to carry a bag of meat as the natives across the lake last winter had done. Since the hides were wanted intact, the men would have to use their shirts as bags. The women would carry the bows and arrows, walking close to the owners in case a quick exchange was needed. Pall was left with the honor of carrying the heavy cowhide himself. This was a day that he would not soon forget.

The trek back to the river took longer than the outward trip, since everyone was tired from the butchering and walking. Two rest stops were necessary before they again came to the Red River. Though the men had kept watch all along the homeward trek, not one person of the group had seen the young native man, Falcon, who had been watching and stealthily following them since the hour they had climbed the low ridge. The Norge recrossed the river to the village, where everyone that had not gone hunting turned out to greet the returning hunters, waiting eagerly to hear the details of the hunt.

Falcon--dressed in a buckskin shirt, breechcloth, moccasins, and leggings up to the calf--sat in the tall grass and watched the activity of the strange men and women in the village across the river. He hadn't been able to get close enough in the open prairie to see their features in much detail, but he had been able to distinguish red, yellow, brown, and black hair. In addition, the faces of the men were covered with hair. They were the strangest sight that he had ever seen.

He had not been present when the large canoes had passed his village on their way up the river, but for days afterward, they had been the main topic of conversation among those that had seen them. His curiosity had been piqued the moment he had heard of the great canoes with the many oars, each one of them, it was said, carrying enough people to populate a small village. When the villagers had described the strangers, he found it difficult to believe that men could possibly look so different. All the people that he had ever seen looked much the same: dark complexions, black hair, and brown eyes. The descriptions of the newcomers, he could now see, were not exaggerations after all.

Scouts from the village had followed the boats at a discreet distance to find out where the pale strangers were going, and what they were up to. Even after the strangers had settled down, a constant vigil had been maintained, but no contact had been attempted. Falcon's curiosity was stronger than his fear of these people. He would keep watch on them for a couple of days, himself, before going back home.

That there were only a few slices of dried meat in his deerskin pouch bothered Falcon not at all. There was food to be had if one but knew where to look, and since he had become a young man, he had lived off the land for many days at a stretch. Several times he had gone two days and more without any food at all, just to test himself.

Although it was still an hour before dark, the freshly harvested bison meat was stored for the night, and all the Norge gathered at the center of the village to hear the recounting of the hunt. There were many exclamations of awe as the vastness of the herd was related. Some of the older members who had never seen a herd closed their eyes and tried to imagine what innumerable animals as far as the eye could see would look like. When the story came to Pall's adventure, there was much good-natured banter, but Pall didn't think any of it was very funny. Much to his embarrassment, he was physically forced by two burly men to show the crowd his torn trousers. He knew in his heart that this story would be told repeatedly, making him the brunt of endless jokes, until the day he died. He wasn't missed when an hour later he put his bow and a few pieces of roasted meat, along with the bison hide, into one of the boats and crossed back over the river.

Falcon, who had gotten his name because of his extraordinarily sharp vision, watched intently as the pale skinned youth made his way to a nearby grove of trees, spread the cow hide, hair side up, and lay down on it, muttering angrily to himself until he finally went to sleep. As darkness was falling, Falcon silently crept to within a few feet of the strange, yellow-haired boy. Sitting with his back against a tree, knees drawn up, he laid his head on his forearms and in a few short minutes was also fast asleep.

When Pall awoke the next morning, a few seconds of panic elapsed before he remembered where he was. He sat up quickly, looked around, and almost cried out as he looked over his shoulder into the darkest eyes he had ever seen, gazing intently at him. His first impulse was to grab for the knife at his belt, but the sheath was empty. Without turning his head, he felt for his bow and quiver; they too were gone. With panic mounting within, Pall braced himself for an attack, but the swarthy person beside him said something unintelligible and with a smile, offered him the missing knife, handle first.

Pall, trying to force a smile, thanked the young man, and with shaking hands, resheathed the knife. Afterward, when he was offered the bow and quiver, he began to relax, thinking that maybe he wasn't going to die after all. He sat for a few seconds in silence, feeling slightly embarrassed because he didn't know what to do next. Then, the native man, pointing in the direction that the group of hunters had gone yesterday, broke the silence with a long speech interspersed with sign language. Pall had no idea what was being said until the youth made motions with his arms like an animal running. When the young man laughed and tossed his head, with index fingers held above his temples like horns, then pointed at his backside, Pall knew exactly what he was referring to.

"Good God in heaven!" Pall exclaimed. "Not you, too. I came across the river to escape this very thing. Did everybody in the world see what happened yesterday? Is there no place I can go where fun won't be poked at me?" he asked, waving his hands in frustration as he ranted.

The native youth seemed to understand that he had touched a sore spot and tried to make amends as best he could. Not knowing what else to do, he lifted a corner of the bison hide, and with scraping motions, told Pall that unless the hide was scraped and dried it would be stinking soon. Pall understood and nodded his agreement, a little too vigorously. The conversation had come to a pause again, when Falcon abruptly stood and pointed at a boat coming across the river. He picked up his bow and turned to go, but Pall stopped him.

"Wait. You don't have to go. That is my father coming to look for me. I left yesterday without telling anyone where I was going. He won't do you any harm. Come on, sit back down," coaxed Pall, as he patted the hide.

Falcon understood not a word that was said, but he was convinced by Pall's tone of voice that no harm would befall him. He sat down and waited.

Pall was subdued in spirit as his father, Gudni, made his way toward the grove of trees. He hadn't even considered until now how his parents might have worried about him. His only thought was to distance himself from the fun-making crowd. He might have acted rashly last night by leaving the compound, but he wouldn't stand for another scolding, if that were his father's intention. He wasn't a full-grown man yet, but he certainly was no longer a child either.

When Pall's father saw that Pall wasn't alone, his hand unconsciously went to his dagger, but he made no threatening move. He noticed that the young native man with his son was tensed for fight or flight, so he stopped some feet away. In one glance, his eyes took in everything about the young native--the stone knife at his waist, the bow and quiver of arrows lying near his feet, the right leg drawn up ready to spring. "Pall, your mother and I were worried about you, Son. We could see the boat from the other side of the river. Is everything all right?" he asked, taking his eyes off Falcon for the first time.

"Yes, Father, everything is just fine. I was just about ready to come back home. It wasn't necessary for you to come looking for me."

"Well, obviously, I didn't know that. Who is your friend?" asked Gudni, as he removed his hand from his dagger.

"I don't know his name yet. We haven't gotten that far. We met only a short while ago."

"Are you ready to go back now? Your mother has made a stew of bison meat seasoned with wild garlic and other herbs. It smelled wonderful, and I'm hungry enough to eat a raw fish."

"Can...uh...my friend...go with us? I mean, that is, if he wants to."

"Yes, of course. He seems harmless enough. He is alone, isn't he?"

"I think so. I haven't seen anyone else." Pall turned to Falcon and, rubbing his stomach, pointed across the river. "Are you hungry?" he asked while making eating motions.

Falcon understood and nodded his acceptance without hesitation. He was excited, though a little apprehensive, at the prospect of going to the strange village--mostly excited. The native scouts had been afraid even to let themselves be seen by the newcomers, and here he was being invited into their village. Not one of his people would find it easy to believe that he, who was not yet a warrior, could accomplish such a feat. Yes, he would go with the pale faces. Judging from the information that had been gathered, these strangers had tools and weapons, the likes of which, his people had never seen before. What a glorious opportunity this was. The warriors in his village would be so envious. He was ecstatic, but no one would have guessed by looking at his face.

Falcon could only guess at the identity of the older man. That he was the father of Pall was the only reasonable deduction. Both had the same golden colored hair, the color of birch leaves in the fall, and the same blue eyes that for some reason reminded him of the icy cold of winter. He shivered within, not because he was cold, but at the thought that he might be walking into a trap. What if these blue-eyed strangers ate human flesh, as was said of his enemies the Ojibway? Well, it was too late to back down without appearing cowardly. He would stay close to the yellow-haired youth, and if anyone tried to lay a hand on him, he would stab the pale skinned youth in the throat with his stone knife. If he were to die, he would take at least one of them with him.

Falcon stepped into Pall's boat as gingerly as he would have had it been a canoe. He could see at once that such care was unnecessary, as the boat had a wide hull and was very stable. His people could never have made such a craft as this with the stone tools they had available. Though the technology to build this boat far exceeded his own, what possible advantage could such a boat have over a canoe? A canoe was light and could be rowed with all ease, while facing forward. Both Pall and his father were struggling mightily against the current, with an oar in each hand, while facing rearward. How awkward that must be.

There was a large crowd of curious people gathered at the riverbank to see whom the figure in the boat with Pall could be. Falcon gripped his bow a little tighter as he walked close behind Pall up the slope toward the waiting crowd. Everyone--men, women, and children—were talking at once, making Falcon think of a gaggle of geese. His confidence was steadily growing, as no one as yet had shown the least sign of hostility, only curiosity. Well, he could understand that; he was blessed--or cursed—with a curious mind himself.

Gudni stopped to explain as best as he could to the crowd, allowing Pall and Falcon the freedom to continue unhindered to the lodge. Bowls were filled, but in deference to Gudni, Pall, his mother, and Falcon patiently waited for Gudni's presence before eating. Respect for the head of the household was a custom that Falcon well understood and practiced at home. When Gudni was seated, the family members bowed their heads, while Falcon watched, and Gudni mumbled something unintelligible before they began to eat.

They ate in silence, but as soon as everyone was finished, Pall began to try to communicate with Falcon. Pointing his finger at his own chest, he repeated his name until Falcon made a similar sound. "Yes! Yes, that is good," exclaimed Pall. In the same manner, Pall introduced his father and mother, saying their names until Falcon could repeat them, and then indicated to Falcon that it was his turn. After hearing the name, Pall tried to get the same guttural sound to come from the back of his own throat. His mother and father were doing no better than he was in producing the sound. All three sounded as if they were clearing their throats.

Looking around the lodge, Falcon spotted a short piece of plank salvaged from the dismantling of the ships. Thora, Pall's mother, had been using the plank as a cutting board when preparing meals. Fetching the board and a piece of charcoal from the hearth, Falcon began to sketch an image. When he had finished, he turned the board so that the other three could see the drawing. Pointing at the image, then at himself, Falcon again made the sound of his name.

"That's a bird," said Pall. "Surely his name is not bird."

"Looks like a hawk or eagle to me," said Thora.

"No, I am sure that he has drawn a falcon," said Gudni. "Look at the configuration of the body and the details that he has added. It 's really a very good likeness."

"Well, since his name is so difficult for us to say, let's just call him Falcon, whether the sketch is a falcon or not." All three pointed at the sketch and said in unison: "Falcon."

Grinning, Falcon nodded his head and tapped his chest with his index finger, repeated, as best he could, the sound they had made. Even though he didn't know what they had said, he decided to take the easy way and accept the name, whatever it meant.

VI

Pall and Falcon became the best of friends. During the next two days they were inseparable, doing everything together. When it came to competing with the other young men, they always did it as a team. Falcon was by far the fastest runner, the best swimmer, and the best marksman with a bow, but some of the bigger and stronger Norge boys were better at wrestling, weightlifting, and other activities that required sheer strength. Only two of the Norge boys showed any resentment at being bested in the contests by an outsider, but that was to be expected. It was the same way among Falcons own people.

Working with the adult men in the fashioning of wolf traps gave Falcon a sense of importance that he had never felt before. The Norge seemed to care not at all that he was yet a youngster. His knowledge of hunting bison and trapping wolves, skills the Norge had never developed as Greenlanders, made him their equal.

He was having so much fun that the days passed much too quickly. There was so much to learn, so many interesting things to do. The tools and weapons of the Norge he found fascinating. Some things, such as felling trees by fire, took many hours for his people to accomplish but were done by the iron tools of the Norge in minutes. He would like to stay with his new friend until he was fully ready to return home, but his people would be concerned about his welfare and might do something rash, thinking that he might have been taken hostage by these strangers.

Falcon had already stayed with the Norge longer than he had intended. His original plan was to watch the village from across the river, never once dreaming that he would actually enter the homes of these strange people. And how strange they were; yet he had grown to like several of them as much as some of the people of his own tribe. He had come to realize that these strangers were merely human beings who wanted the same things that others wanted—food, clothing, shelter, and happiness. There was nothing sinister about them, as he had imagined there might be before he had gotten to know them.

During the days of his sojourn, Falcon had picked up several Norge words and phrases—enough that he could make Pall understand that he must return to his own home before long. Pall had picked up a few words from Falcon, but the learning was mostly one-sided, since the burden was on Falcon as the outsider. Besides, he wanted to learn as much as possible about this new race of people, and he could learn much faster if he knew the language.

Early the next morning, after eating breakfast and while the family of Pall was together, Falcon announced he must go home. "Falcon go. Pall go Falcon," he said matter of factly.

Pall, taken by surprise and not knowing what to say, looked pleadingly at his father.

"This is certainly an unexpected development," said Gudni. "Would Pall be safe, Falcon?"

"Falcon, with own life…" Falcon began, but he didn't know the right word to finish.

"Are you trying to say that you would defend Pall with your own life," asked Gudni.

"Yes," agreed Falcon. "With own life Falcon defend Pall."

"Do you want to go, Pall?" asked Thora.

"Yes. I think it would be very educational as well as interesting," said Pall. "Since we are going to live in this land, we need to learn all we can about the native people. Don't you agree, Father?"

"It is agreed then. Will you try to be back in seven days or so? I wouldn't want your mother to worry for too long," Gudni said, knowing full well that Thora wouldn't be the only one concerned.

"I promise. What should I take with me, Falcon? My bow and knife?"

"No! No weapon. No need weapon," said Falcon. "Falcon like knife. What take?"

"After the way you have worked with us making wolf traps and snares, I should have given you a knife already. Here, you can have the one I carry. I have others," said Gudni, handing Falcon the knife, handle first.

Falcon held the knife with reverence in his open palms, his face aglow. "Falcon much like."

Without further delay, Pall and Falcon loaded a few items into one of the boats, and Gudni rowed the young men to the other side of the river. Falcon jumped ashore before the boat quite touched land and never looked back until he reached the grove of trees at the top of the slope. Gudni and Pall clasped each other in a quick embrace, and then Pall hurried after Falcon. Both of the young men waved goodbye before turning to disappear over the rise.

Gudni stood for several minutes staring at the spot where he had last seen the boys. He wondered if he would ever see his son again. It was a natural thing for a parent to worry about a child, and especially in this case, for Pall, having led a sheltered life, had never been away from home before. It was time, though, to loosen the apron strings. Gudni supposed that Pall would be a much different person when he returned home; it was time for the man-child to become a man.

Gudni was subdued with melancholia when he returned to the village. He could tell at a glance that Thora had been crying during his short absence. Her eyes were red and swollen, and smoke stains from the breakfast fire were smeared across her cheeks. Gudni knew that he had to find a task with which to busy himself or he would surely become depressed. The village hunters had been so intent on building and setting wolf traps the past week that no one had even thought about taking the fishing boats to the lake country to the east. That would be a good project to begin with. Thora may be interested in getting away for a couple of days. A short excursion would do them both good. He immediately began a circuit through the village, asking for volunteers. Before he was halfway through, there were more than enough willing hands to man the boats.

Because he had never been to the lake region, Steinn decided to go along. He hadn't been outside the compound for over a month and was ready for a diversion.

Various hunting parties had already explored the country east of the Red River for at least twenty leagues from the village. Many small lakes had been discovered that were teeming with fish. It would be an easy matter to row the boats to the lake drained by the Bison River, but some of the boats would have to be dragged to other destinations, as navigatable streams did not connect all the lakes. There was some concern that the boats would not be safe if left at the lakes unguarded, but there was no solution for that problem. They would have to be hidden as well as possible and left to chance.

The natives had no permanent villages in the immediate vicinity of the lakes, but Norge hunting parties had often found evidence of their visitations. Footprints and campfire ashes were common signs, and fleeting glimpses were sometimes caught of half-naked bodies ducking for cover, but no personal contact was ever made. Not one of the Norge hunting parties had ever been threatened, and nothing, not even the wolf traps, had been molested. Steinn was adamant in his belief that the natives as well as their possessions should always be treated with the same respect; the very existence of the Norge depended on the goodwill of the surrounding tribes. Maybe, at least he hoped, the boats would not be bothered as well.

All the boats except two were loaded with fishing equipment and enough food to last two days. Hunting parties, needing to cross the Red River, could use the remaining two boats. Gudni had persuaded Thora to come with him on the excursion, convincing her that the outing would be good for her. Rolf was taking Helga, as if he had another choice, in one of the other boats. As they got under way, there were a total of ten boats with forty people in them, strung out on the river, with Steinn in the lead.

Since it was mid-morning when they had started, they had to make camp when little more than halfway to their destination. Rowing against the current was always slow, and the Bison River, though small, was quite swift in places. Once they had the boats distributed among the several lakes, the people would have to walk from the lakes back to the village. The journey back should take no longer than the rowing against the current on the outward journey. The boats would be permanent fixtures on the lakes, until they decayed or were destroyed. The plan was to dry the fish caught at the lakes and carry them back to the village. This time plenty of baskets had been brought along.

The destination was attained during the middle of the second day. The men, tired from rowing, plopped down in the grass on the lakeshore and awaited the meal being prepared by Helga and Thora. They were glad that the women had decided to come along on the trip. It seemed that food always tasted better when prepared by a female, at least that was what they told themselves. No one knew exactly why, but Helga's meals had a particular flavor that set them apart from Norge cooking and were greatly preferred by some of the men, Rolf in particular. She was now fully conformed to Norge society and was no longer considered an outsider by anyone, in fact, she no longer thought of herself as being anything but Norge. Her life as a child in the Beothuk village was fast becoming a dim memory.

The fishing boats were launched after everyone had eaten and rested. The nets were cast, and since the lake had never before been fished in this manner, the result was large catches almost immediately. The fishermen would watch the surface of the lake for schools of minnows fleeing from predators, and then encircle the area with their nets. The minnows would escape through the net, leaving the bigger fish entrapped.

Fires were built, and while some of the men prepared the fish for curing, others tended the drying racks or chopped wood. So many fish were taken that a change of plans was forthcoming. After the fish were smoked and dried, it was decided that two of the boats would be hidden in a large patch of wild grain that was growing in the shallow water near the shore, and the other eight boats would be loaded with fish for the return trip. Distributing boats among the other lakes would have to wait

The food brought from the village had lasted for two days, as planned, but on the third day, the women went searching for edible plants to supplement the fish that had already been taken. There were cattails in abundance growing in the shallows, and at this time of the year, the new shoots were tender and nourishing. With boiled cattail roots, tender green shoots, and plentiful fish, there was no shortage of food.

The wild grain growing in the shallows was something new to the Norge. Some of it would have to be harvested in the fall to see if it was edible. Maybe it would be suitable for the making of bread.

With all the dried fish, there was not enough room for everyone in the heavily laden boats, so Steinn, Rolf, and several other men decided to turn the return trip into a hunting opportunity. Rolf had to be very persuasive, since he and Helga had been inseparable until now, but at last he prevailed in convincing her to make the boat trip home, while he walked back. For those in the boats, the journey down the river was easy and swift.

The fishing trip had been successful in diverting the minds of Gudni and Thora away from Pall, but now that they were home again, the realization that their son was at another village, a village of strangers, came crashing back. The outing, with the time taken to dry the fish, had lasted five days. Pall had promised to stay no longer than a week. Somehow, they would have to occupy themselves for two long days and pray that Pall would not extend his visit. Both of them realized that Pall was nearing manhood and would soon be making his own way in the world, but it was the way of parents to hold on to their young as long as possible.

To the great relief of his parents, Pall returned two days later exactly as he had promised. Falcon, as well as another young native man, stood behind Pall as he hailed his father from across the Red River. Gudni, while vainly trying to show nonchalance, eagerly rowed across the river to pick them up. After Gudni had embraced his son, he shook hands with the widely smiling Falcon, but the other young man, separating himself from the others by a few feet, was so nervous and frightened that he appeared about to be sick. The youth, trying to stay as far away as possible from Gudni, reluctantly entered the boat. Pall explained as they crossed the river that the youngster was actually the son of the village chief. The fact that the young man was present at all showed the great esteem that the village now held for Falcon.

Falcon had presented the skinning knife that Gudni had given him, a most prized possession and one that he would have liked to keep for himself, as a gift to the village chief, telling him that it was a gift from the chief of the Norge. In this way he hoped to forge a feeling of goodwill between the two races.

Soon after Pall and Falcon had entered the native village, the elders had been called to a meeting, and after relating all that he had learned about the white man's village, Falcon was treated with much respect by the older men. Although he had not yet under-gone the rites of manhood, he had accomplished a deed that none of the village warriors had shown a willingness to do.

Since the coming of the pale strangers, the village spies had maintained a constant watch around the compound, but from a safe distance, as the hairy giants felled large trees in a matter of minutes. After studying the stumps and large chips thrown off by the axes, the spies were convinced that the Norge were using magic tools in the cutting of the logs. They watched in awe as limbs were severed from the tree trunks with a single blow. Some of the bits of information carried back to the village were so fantastic that they were treated as exaggerations, until Falcon had presented the metal knife as proof. When the elders of the village witnessed the shavings turned up from a willow branch, the superiority of the stranger's tools was easily seen.

Metal as hard and sharp as this had never before been seen by anyone in the village, not even by the oldest members. There were tales of a pale race that traveled through this area generations ago on its way south, but few believed the stories were based on fact. But now, with the arrival of the Norge, even the skeptics believed. Since there were open mines a few days journey to the east, copper implements and ornaments were common in the surrounding area, but iron was something strangely new and wonderful. The chief held the knife reverently, as if it were an object of worship.

The gift of the knife, as well as bringing Pall to the village with him, had made Falcon an instant celebrity. For days, until he had answered a thousand questions about the strange people who had settled upstream, he had hardly any privacy. Representatives of the *Ocheti Shakowin*, the Seven Council Fires, had met during Falcon's absence to discuss the intruders, but the meeting had adjourned without coming to a firm decision. Some leaders had wanted to go to war with the strangers and drive them from the land, but others were afraid that war would be disastrous, especially if the strangers used magic weapons. Now that Falcon had been allowed inside the Norge village, why act in haste? Much needed information could be gathered to help in making a decision. The Seven Council Fires would have the advantage with what they considered a spy in the stranger's camp.

Falcon realized the position of importance that was about to be thrust upon him. He was fascinated by the pale strangers and wanted to learn everything possible about them. He had come to realize the Norge were simply people who wanted to live and raise a family, just as the Sisseton sept, of which he was a member. It was his intention to do everything within his power to prevent war, even if he had to exaggerate the power of his newfound friends. Even with their iron weapons, Falcon knew that the Norge would be no match for the combined force of the Seven Council Fires.

When Falcon had disappeared on the day of the bison hunt, it was feared by his people that the hairy strangers had taken him, but then the startling news had been brought back by one of the spies that Falcon had been seen inside the Norge compound, apparently free and unharmed. Without them even knowing it, this fact had weighed heavily in the stranger's favor. Why wage war against a people, it was argued by some, when they obviously meant no harm. This was a vast land; there was more than enough territory and game for everyone, including the pale skins, that is, if they remained peaceful. And besides, if the axes and swords of the strangers were as fearsome as Falcon had, upon his return, portrayed them, it would be much too costly to wage war without a very good reason.

For the present it was decided, with some dissention, the status quo would be maintained. If the pale skins molested any member of the seven septs, another meeting would be called immediately. If the food supply began to fail, the strangers would have to go. Falcon agreed to continue to be the main liaison between the two parties.

Falcon's decision to be in the middle wasn't entirely unselfish. True, he had been born a Sisseton Lakota, and had his nation's best interest at heart, but there was also a certain redhaired Norge maiden that had caught his eye, giving him more reason for keeping the peace between the two factions. Fact being, he would now rather be inside the Norge compound than to be in his own village.

The relationship between Falcon and the Norge was drawing ever closer. Not only was he transferring his knowledge of hunting and trapping to those who wanted to learn, but also, he was learning things that he had never dreamed about. The leader of the Norge, the one called Steinn, was building a furnace, the likes of which Falcon had never seen before. In this furnace, called a kiln, wood was changed into charcoal, which burned, by the means of forced air, much hotter than untreated wood. A forge, with a funnel underneath to increase the airflow through the charcoal, made it possible to heat iron white hot. The large end of the skin-covered funnel was flexible enough to be turned several degrees in order to better catch the prevailing wind. Steinn showed Falcon how broken tools and weapons could be repaired by heating and hammering the hot metal back together again.

There was no attempt to actually turn ore into iron, as Steinn had done in Vinland, but unless the life of the present supply of metal was extended, the Norge would someday be dependent on stone implements, as were the natives of this land. In exchange for the lessons in metallurgy, Falcon taught those interested in the working of stone how to shape arrow and spear points from flint. Steinn was surprised to learn that stone was easier to work with if heat-treated before chipping. His knowledge of metalworking helped him to become quite adept at flint knapping. Pall also showed much promise in learning this skill.

Steinn seemed pleased that Falcon was interested in learning everything possible about life in the compound. There were some who thought it dangerous to let a native acquire so much knowledge about their way of life, but Steinn seemed to be able to sense a person's true nature. There was no evil intent in Falcon's curiosity, Steinn was sure. He had been right about Floki; he felt he was also right about Falcon.

Copper in free nugget form had long been familiar to the native peoples in the Great Lakes region. Trinkets, baubles, and other ornaments made of beaten copper were a common sight. The making of an intricately designed ornament was a long and tedious process, since the artisan worked with stone tools. After Falcon learned that individual pieces of copper could be melted into one mass in the forge that Steinn had made, and then poured into a clay mold to make almost any form desired, his life was changed forever.

After weeks of trading and gathering every piece of copper he could find, Falcon was able to form a single ingot of about three pounds of pure metal. With Steinn's guidance, he fashioned a mold in the form of a simple wedge-shaped axe head. Falcon held the copper ingot in an iron ladle over the forge, while Steinn stood by ready to help. When the copper became liquidized, he poured the mold full of the molten metal. He was as nervous as an expectant father waiting to see his newborn son, as he waited for the metal to solidify.

When the mold was broken, Falcon was completely devastated at what he beheld. Instead of a shiny copper axe head, there was only a dull lump of something that looked like stone. Steinn laughed because of the dejected look on Falcon's face, as he reached for the axe head. Going to the bench-mounted circular grindstone that had been brought all the way from Greenland, Steinn asked Falcon to turn the hand crank while he held the axe head against the stone. With the removal of the thin patina layer, shiny metal began to appear. Falcon's face glowed brighter than the newly exposed copper. Steinn laughed harder than ever as he handed the roughly finished axe head to a jubilant Falcon.

There was still much work to be done before the axe would be completed. Falcon ground the metal smooth before using a hand-held stone to polish it. Next, he fashioned an ornate handle with a snake's head carved at the end. An appropriately shaped hole was made through the other end to accept the axe head. He then put a wrist thong through the end of the handle. The finished product was a beautiful, shiny axe that was bound to catch the eye of any warrior. The axe was never meant to be utilitarian; the metal was too soft. It was merely a beautiful ornament. If he ever decided to trade it, he was sure to reap a nice profit for his handiwork.

The tools that Falcon used in the making of the axe made the task much easier than if he had used the more primitive methods of the natives. The results would have been the same, but it would have taken much longer and involved more tedious labor. When he studied the construction of the circular grinding stone, he saw the simplicity of its design and wondered why no one in his village had ever thought of making one like it. The funnel at the forge was not so complicated, after one understood the principle of its design, but the making of charcoal was an entirely different matter. How could anyone have ever known that smoldering green wood would render a product that burned much hotter than ordinary wood? Some things simply had to be accepted, if not understood.

The making of the copper axe had given Falcon such a feeling of satisfaction that he was now gathering copper to make an ornate spear with a point a foot long. Of course, when he went to visit his people, he could never take his handiwork with him. For one of his age and status, ownership of such objects would only cause resentment and hostility among those of warrior status, even though they were made with his own hands. Here, among the Norge, he was accepted as an equal despite never having undergone the ordeal of the Sundance, or the fasting for a vision, or the seeking for a spirit guide. As yet, he didn't know enough about Norge customs to understand what made a Norge boy into a man, but it seemed to be a gradual process, rather than a onetime ritual.

As the days became cooler, all thoughts in the compound were turned to laying away stores for the winter. Another fishing trip was planned to what now was referred to as Bison Lake. Extra baskets would be taken along, since Falcon had assured the Norge women that the wild grain growing at the edge of the lake was indeed edible. In the Ojibway tongue it was *mah-no-min*. The Norge had never seen such grain before and had no name for it. They simply called it grain.

Scouts were also sent daily across the Muddy River to watch for the migrating bison herd. With a supply of dried fish, as much grain as they could harvest, and hopefully a successful bison hunt, no one would go hungry. Of course, an occasional deer or moose might be taken at any time during the winter months to augment the food supply.

The fish harvest was once again a great success, and many baskets were filled with the ripened wild rice, which was quite different from wheat, millet, oats or barley. The flat cakes that resulted from the attempts at bread making served the same purpose but couldn't be called bread in the true sense. Nevertheless, the grain was a welcome addition to their diet.

Since the rice grew in shallow water, boats were used in the harvesting of it. The natives, according to Falcon, used canoes, which went between the stalks, causing little destruction. The wide boats of the Norge rode some of the stalks over, but there was no help for it.

Falcon demonstrated to the women how a stick two feet long could be used to draw the stalks over the boat with the left arm, and a light rap from another stick held in the right hand would loosen the mature grains to fall into the boat. As all the seeds did not ripen at the same time, the same areas were harvested twice in one week, using the same boat trails previously made through the stalks. Plenty of seeds were left on the plants for the making of next year's crop.

Some of the grain was cleaned of husks and cooked and served with blueberries, while geese, ducks, and fish rounded out the menu. It had been a festive occasion, and no one wanted to return to the tasks at hand. Steinn, too, was sated to the point of laziness and called for an afternoon of rest before packing for the return trip home.

Steinn found a place of solitude near where the boats were moored, and with his back against a large boulder, he closed his eyes and enjoyed the warm rays of the afternoon sun. Life in this new land was good, and he had no regrets at all about leaving Greenland, but the lack of security worried him greatly. Try as he might, he could not come up with a solution to the problem. He was thinking of a way to forge a bond of friendship and trust with the surrounding tribes, when he realized that he wasn't alone. Though he had heard no sound, when he opened his eyes, there was Falcon standing beside him.

"Is there something you would like to talk about, Steinn? I have noticed that you seem to be worried about something."

"Yes, Falcon," said Steinn, as he regained his feet. "There is something bothering me. Look at this hole that we used to anchor the boats. Have you seen other holes like this in other locations?"

"Yes, there are many such and in many different places.

"Do you know who made them?"

"Made them? I thought they were natural. I did not know they were made."

"My people have been making such holes to use as boat moorings for hundreds of years. I am convinced that some of my ancestors walked this very ground that we are standing on. Are there any legends among your people that tell of an ancient pale skinned race that passed through this area?"

"The Winnebago, the grandfather tribe of many kindred tongues, seem to have a vague remembrance of such a people. When I was a child, I heard an old storyteller mention a pale, hairy race of people that once lived in this area, but the story was dismissed from my mind as mere fantasy, until you and your people came."

"But even today, there are occasional rumors that filter into this area from far away to the southeast about a war being waged by the Shawano tribe against a pale skinned race of people. That is in the valley of the Beautiful River, which flows into the Father of Waters far to the south. Years ago, before my birth I am told, there were the same sort of rumors about another such war even farther away. The pale skins were driven out of that country, also, and now live somewhere along the Great Smoking River to the southwest of here."

"Are you saying there are people of my race living somewhere far to the south of us at this very moment?" asked Steinn, incredulously.

"The stories are not detailed, but the tellers say that the Shawano seem to be slowly driving the pale ones westward out of the valley of the Beautiful River.

"That is the very reason that I am worried, Falcon. With your help as The-One-Who- Goes-Between, there has been a tenuous peace maintained between our peoples, but that peace could be shattered by the least infraction on our part. The Norge could possibly win a battle, but we could never survive a war. There are too few of us."

"How long do you think it would take to make a round trip to the country of these pale skins? I would like to know if we are of the same heritage."

"Would you leave this area to go live with the others if they are of the same blood?" Falcon wondered.

"Yes, I think so."

"I have never made a long journey, and I do not know how far it is to the Beautiful River, but when next I visit my village, I will try to find the answer for you."

"There is strength in numbers. If the majority of my people were agreeable, I would consider joining with the others. Believe me, it is a comfort just knowing that there are others of my race in this vast land. If we were fully accepted by the surrounding tribes, I would be happy to stay right here, forever, but we are strangers in this land, and as such are held in suspicion by the natives of the area. It is only natural they should feel that way about us, but I assure you, we want only to live in peace."

"I know this is true, and I do my best to convince my people of this truth, but there are some who will always want war, no matter what. Some people hate anything that is different and want to destroy it."

"It is the same with all races. I have struggled with the same problem among my own people, and I have made much progress. With you and Helga as good examples, I am happy to say that there is very little prejudice any more amongst the Norge."

"I know that is true. I feel as much at home with your people as with my own. Some in my village say that I have become more Norge than Lakota. That I have changed in certain ways cannot be denied. One thing in particular weighs heavily on my mind, causing me much stress."

"Would it help to talk about it?"

"I am not so sure that talk will help, but neither will it do any harm. You see, the problem is what makes a boy into a man. Among the Lakota, when a boy reaches a certain age, he must find a secluded place where he can fast and pray and seek a vision. Some are fortunate enough to receive a vision the first time; others must repeat the ordeal. A spirit helper in the form of an animal or bird will reveal itself and will guide the person throughout his life."

"Then, one must endure the Sun Dance to show his bravery and disdain for pain. Skewers, attached to rawhide ropes, are put through the skin of the chest or back, and tension is put on the ropes until the day is gone or the holds tear out of the skin."

"I have reached that age and should have gone through those two ordeals this past summer, but playing the part of One-Who-Goes-Between took too much of my time. That is why some say that I have become a pale skin."

"I have lived with you and your people off and on for the whole summer, and I have never heard of an initiation ritual. How does a Norge boy become a man?"

"Actually, there is no single thing one must endure to become a man. It is a gradual process. A boy takes upon himself the responsibilities of an adult until he is considered an adult. There is no certain age that this takes place. Some boys mature much earlier than others. Each one must decide for himself when he has become a man, usually by taking a wife and beginning a family."

"What I am going to tell you has nothing to do with becoming a man, but there is something of a parallel, especially in reference to the spirit guide that you mentioned. In our religion is the belief that there is no remission of sin without the shedding of blood. There was a time when animal sacrifice was acceptable, but then there came a man, whom we believe in as the Son of God, who willingly suffered and died for all mankind. Because He shed His blood, we don't have to shed ours. He was nailed to a cross for our sins. If we accept His suffering in our stead, His spirit within us becomes our guide. To suffer unnecessarily is foreign to our way of thinking."

"I do not understand any of this."

"What I am saying," said Steinn, "is that we depend on God's Holy Spirit to guide us from within; whereas you seek a spirit helper, usually in the form of an animal, to guide you. Isn't that right?"

"Yes, that is correct, but in a crisis, we will ask the spirit guide to appear in live form to help us. Your ways are strange to me. I do not understand this being guided from within. Maybe we can discuss this farther at another time."

"Yes, it grows late, and we must pack the boats for the trip home. We will set out at daybreak, with the women in the boats and most of the men hunting on the way back, just as we have done before."

The boats were so filled with fish and grain, that again no attempt was made to distribute the boats among the various lakes, but as long as Bison Lake alone furnished their requirements, there was no need to fish the other lakes.

The journey home was uneventful, and after the boats were unloaded at the compound, Falcon demonstrated to the women how to spread the rice harvest on bison skins to dry. Days later he dug a hole in the ground, lined it with a bison skin, and poured in some of the dry grain. Wearing soft deer skin moccasins so as not to crush the seeds, he trampled the husks from the rice, stirring the seed occa-sionally with a foot, so that all of the grains would be exposed to the trampling. After the husks had been loosened, two strong men lifted the skin from the hole, and the grain was carefully tossed into the air to allow the wind to blow away the chaff. The rice was now ready for storage.

A few days after the return of the fishermen, a great bison herd, slowly migrating southward, was spotted to the west. The villagers that had missed the first hunt were given the chance to attend. Only those too old, too young, or too ill turned the oppor-tunity down.

The people who had seen the first bison herd were awed anew at the sight of so many animals in one place. Surely such a great herd of animals was inexhaustible. Considering the number of calves that would be born next year, the number of harvested animals was negligible. There should be enough meat for all the inhabitants of the land, forever.

Wearing the wolf skins in the style of the natives made stalking the animals much easier. The hunt was a huge success, producing more than enough meat to last through the winter.

With preparations for the winter completed, Falcon left the Norge compound to visit his people for a few days. As time progressed, his visits home were getting to be fewer and farther between. The attitude of the villagers had changed noticeably toward him. He was no longer greeted with the warmth that he had known in the past, as there seemed to be a gulf forming between him and his once close companions. Even his own family were becoming as strangers to him. Some of the villagers were even beginning to question his loyalty to the tribe.

It was difficult to concentrate on the everyday village chatter and gossip because his mind was usually back with the Norge, wondering what adventures Pall was up to, what interesting contraption Steinn might be working on, or if the pretty red haired girl was showing too much interest in some other young man. He could hardly wait to get back to the compound, but he had to stay at least a few days with his people, just for appearance sake. At the first possible chance he would make his excuse to leave. Somewhere in the back of his mind was the germ of a thought that he refused to let surface. He wasn't ready to admit to himself that he was fast becoming more Norge than Sisseton.

It wasn't difficult to get the information Steinn wanted, since much of the conversations he participated in centered on the

Norge. Asking questions about the pale skins in the far south fell right into place. No one among the adult men in the village doubted that such a people existed, and the talk of war between the Shawano tribe and the pale skins along the Beautiful River fed the hopes of those that wanted war with the Norge.

As falcon helped his family gather the maize crop, he managed to sneak a double handful of the largest kernels into a small skin bag and hid it inside his shirt. He did the same with a single handful of dried squash seed. He didn't ask for the seeds openly because he was sure that his family, as well as the tribe, would not want to share with the Norge in this way.

Falcon had been somewhat depressed since the day of his arrival in his home village, but his spirits rose dramatically the day he decided to go back to the Norge compound. He tried to hide his jubilation as he said his goodbyes, but the moment the village was out of sight, he broke into a running and jumping fit. Though he had never been a prisoner, he now felt as if he had been set free.

He ran a while, and he walked a while; he ran a while, and he walked a while. He kept this pace until he came to the crossing of the river. Instead of hailing the compound and waiting for a boat, he waded into the cold water and swam on his back, holding the precious seed bags above the water, until he was again in the shallows of the opposite shore.

As soon as he waded ashore, he was met by a group of his closest friends, one of them holding a dry skin robe. Maybe he was becoming soft living as a Norge, but the warmth the robe afforded felt good to his cold wet skin. He and Pall greeted each other as if Falcon had been gone for weeks instead of days. Gudni and Thora fussed over him as if he were a prodigal son returned home. Steinn simply shook his hand in greeting and told him to come to his lodge when he found the time.

As soon as he had made his rounds to say hello to all his friends, including the red-haired girl, Falcon made his way to Steinn's lodge. Steinn was sitting on a split-log bench, honing an axe. He moved to allow Falcon room to sit beside him. "I have gathered very little information concerning the land of the Beautiful River," began Falcon, knowing why Steinn had asked him there. "No one of my tribe has ever made such a long journey. All anyone knows is what has been passed from tribe to tribe and probably such information has been distorted in the many retellings. But all agree that the time to make such a journey would be well beyond a year, and all of it, for a pale skin at least, would be through hostile territory. It might be barely possible to move all of the Norge at one time by boat, but even then, word would precede your passing, making the possibility of an ambush likely somewhere along the way."

"Then there is a way to travel by water from here to there?"

"Yes, but it would be much farther than by land, since it would not be a direct route. The headwaters of the great river known as the Father of Waters is a lake only a short distance east of Bison Lake, but there is no way to get boats to the that lake without dragging them over land. But once there, one could continue south to the mouth of the Beautiful River. It is also possible to go to the head of our river, the Red River, and with a short portage gain access to a tributary of the Father of Waters, which flows in the opposite direction as the Red. Then one would continue down stream to the mouth of the Beautiful River."

"Also, there are lakes to the east, the size of which is astounding I am told. If one went by way of these lakes, one could travel by water almost to the Beautiful River country. Getting boats to the lakes would be a problem."

"What if all the pale ones have been driven from the Beautiful River Valley and now reside along the Smoking River? Do you know the best way to the Smoking River from here?" asked Steinn

"I also thought to ask about that possibility. The same river routes just mentioned would also take one even farther south to the mouth of the Smoking River, but then, it would be necessary to make a long journey to the northwest up the Smoking River. No one knows how far up that river the other pale skins traveled before settling down. The most direct route would be to travel up the river just a short way upstream on the other side of the Red. It is known to my people as the Sheyenne River, named for a tribe forced out of this area by the expansion of the Seven Council Fires. There is but one small village remaining on the river. The main body of the tribe has migrated much farther to the west, across the great Smoking River, almost to the Shining Mountains."

"What are the Shining Mountains? My head is already spinning from all these rivers and lakes, and here comes more information to absorb."

"The Shining Mountains are far to the west. Their peaks are always covered with snow. With the light of the sun reflecting off the snow... Well, you get the picture."

"Ah. Yes, I see. Now, to get back to the Sheyenne River."

"The only problem would be dragging the boats over land for possibly two days after the river plays out Would that be possible?"

Steinn pursed his lips in deep concentration for a few seconds before answering. "I do believe that problem could be readily solved by attaching out-rigger skid poles to each side of the boats. That would give them stability, and also less resistance than the wide flat bottoms would create. With ropes attached to the front, there should be more than enough men to pull them. The women and bigger children could push from behind."

"Of course, this discussion is just in case the need to flee ever arises. Everyone is happy here and would like to stay, but one must try to think ahead and be prepared as much as possible. This compound is like a small island in a vast lake, and since we are few in number, my mind is never completely at ease, even though there has been no trouble thus far."

"I believe I like the last suggestion best of all. I will have out-riggers and skid poles made for all the boats and kept ready just in case they are needed. Thank you, Falcon, for the information. You are a great help."

Falcon went to find his best friend and presented to Pall the idea of building their own dwelling. At first Pall was enthusiastic about the prospect of having his own lodge, but after thinking about the cooking and cleaning and other household chores, his spirit became somewhat subdued.

After the subject was broached before his mother and father, Thora assured Pall that if he and Falcon continued to furnish the family with meat that she would be happy to cook enough for all of them. The two young men started immediately gathering logs and saplings for their new dwelling. On the third day, they stood back to admire their handiwork. The lodge wasn't as big and sturdy as most of the other dwellings in the compound, but it would be sufficient for their needs, and they were quite proud of it.

With a strand of rawhide, Falcon suspended the maize bag from the ceiling of the new lodge, so that mice could not get to it. Once they were comfortably settled into their new home, falcon chose an unused open area of the compound as the site for a vegetable garden. Though gardening was the chore of women in his own village, he had no woman to rely on, and besides, things were different with the Norge. In their society, there was no shame in men doing any kind of honest labor, including cooking and gardening.

Falcon, with Pall's help, started preparations for the garden by digging foot deep holes, eighteen inches in diameter, in the ground and filling them with a mixture of dead leaves, wood chips, and ashes from the hearths of the villagers. Every time he and Pall went into the open prairie throughout the rest of the winter, they would bring back a bag each of dried bison chips and crumbled them one at a time into the holes. As each hole was filled, they would cover it with earth to stand and decompose as much as possible until planting time came in the spring.

Pall and Falcon kept busy and enjoyed their new lifestyle so much that spring arrived, it seemed, in record time. Gudni and Thora, as well as Steinn, had kept an eye on the young men throughout the winter and were well pleased with the way they were maturing. Most of the Norge thought of Falcon as one of their own and treated him as if he were the brother of Pall.

When the right time came to plant, plus two weeks extra just as a precaution against the likelihood of frost, Falcon lovingly pushed the maize kernels into the soft ground, five to a mound, saying a short prayer of blessing at each mound, until they were all planted. He did the same with the few squash seeds, though the maize seeds were of more interest to him.

This was the second spring of the Norge sojourn in the new land, and though they were eating well, the most recent fishing expedition to Bison Lake had netted fewer fish than in the past. It was decided to take the two boats to a new location, a much larger lake they named Cormorant Lake a short distance to the south of Bison Lake.

Since there was no river that could be taken to the new lake, it would be necessary to drag the boats overland. This gave Steinn a chance to try his new outrigger devise. Once the boats were outfitted with the outriggers, two ropes were attached to the front of each boat, with a man to each rope. The boats skidded across the grass-covered ground with all ease, making the portage much easier than anticipated. Of course, if fleeing this area ever became necessary, loading the boats with household goods would make them quite a bit heavier.

The only inconvenience in the new site was that all the fish caught would have to be carried back home, rather than taken by boat. But maybe next year the fishing could be resumed for a season at Bison Lake.

The maize plants were soon waist high with the beginnings of tiny ears in the making. The whole village watched as Falcon faithfully tended the plants, pulling weeds, keeping the soil loose, and carrying water from the river when necessary to keep the soil moist. When some weeks later the ears were filled out, Falcon dug a large hole in the ground and built a fire of hickory wood in the bottom. When the fire had burned down to a thick bed of coals, he put in a layer of green leaves. On top of the leaves he put half of the maize crop still in the shuck, filling the hole almost to the top.

Next, Falcon placed another layer of leaves and lastly covered everything with earth, leaving a small opening at the center of the hole. Through the small hole he poured water until steam began to rise from the hole. The ears were steamed this way for at least an hour. By the time the ashes were cooled by the water, the ears of maize were thoroughly cooked. There wasn't enough for everyone to have a full ear, but all got a good taste of the new grain. Everyone agreed that it was delicious, even better than the squash. The remainder of the crop was allowed to mature and kept as seed. Maybe by the third summer, Falcon hoped, anyone that wanted to plant could have enough seed to raise his own crop.

VII

"Eastward ho!"

This cry from the watchtower was the first alarm that had been raised since the Norge village had been founded, but within seconds there were more than two dozen armed men at the palisade wall, with more on the way.

Not until the newcomers were within a hundred yards of the wall were any of them recognized. "Steinn!" yelled a man from the wall. "It's Floki and his crew, but there seems to be an extra man with them."

"Open the gate," ordered Steinn. "Everyone stay alert in case there are others following. Watchman in the tower! Keep an eye all around as best you can. I don't want any surprises."

"Steinn, my man," said Floki, looking right and left as he entered the compound. "I'm touched to know you missed me, but I really didn't expect so many to turn out in greeting, and armed, too," said Floki, much too cheerfully.

"Well, Floki, you'll have to admit that you aren't dressed exactly as you were the last time I saw you, and one of the men with you does appear to be a native."

"Clothes tend to wear out, don't they? You should take a look at yourself. And yes, that savage is Raven Wing, the son of the village chief back where I left my ship. I…well… you know… persuaded the old man to lend me his son as a guide. You needn't concern yourself about him; he's harmless enough."

"It's not him I'm concerned about. If you and your men are hungry, I can get the women to fix you something to eat, and then I want to know why you are here."

"Ha! You certainly don't waste any time, do you? Wouldn't you like to hear about my adventures and discoveries first? Well, I suppose in a way my adventures and purpose for being here are one and the same. I can't tell you what I want without telling you what I've been doing the past few summers."

"All Right. I'll see about getting you and your men refreshed, and then we'll talk. If you will keep everybody together in the shade of that pine tree over there, it will be more convenient for the women to serve you."

"Why, Steinn, I get the feeling you don't trust me and my men."

"I don't. And you had better keep them in good behavior while you are here. We have a tenuous relationship with the natives around here. I won't have anyone upsetting the balance. Is that understood?"

"I think that is plain enough. I didn't come here to start trouble, Steinn. In fact, I would like to mend our differences and try to be a friend to you."

"We'll see about that," said Steinn, as he turned to go.

Before talking to the women, Steinn went to find Rolf. He wanted at least 20 men to be armed at all times while Floki and his crew remained inside the compound. He let Rolf choose his own men, Pall being one of the first chosen.

Rolf had become Steinn's strong right arm. He had come to rely on Rolf and had let him choose a squad of a dozen men as a police force of sorts.

When the newcomers had eaten and most of them were dozing in the shade, Steinn invited Floki to his lodge. They sat on the split log bench beside the lodge door with their backs against the wall and looked out over the compound. It was a peaceful scene as the people went about their everyday affairs, but Steinn had a feeling it wasn't going to stay that way.

"Floki, if you would, start with the day you left the camp on the great lake and tell me everything that has happened since."

"If you think that lake was big, you would be astounded to see the lakes to the east of here. They are like seas. I have been told there are five of them, all connected in a series. I've explored three of them, though not thoroughly, and according to the Scraelings beyond the fourth lake there is a mighty waterfall. The very same one that I have seen before, I'm thinking."

Well, after leaving you at the lake camp, we rowed as far as we could up the river that flows into the big lake from the southeast. I should have known better than to strike out so late in the season, but at the time, I was a little too upset to care. We became entangled in such a maze of lakes and streams that it was impossible to retrace our path before winter caught us. We chose an advantageous campsite on a small lake, took the mast from the ship, turned it upside down, and built a rock wall chinked with moss under the sides. It was cozy enough, but food was kind of scarce at times."

"I'm jumping too far ahead, though. Before we beached the ship, some of us netted as many fish as we possibly could before the lake froze, while others harvested a few moose and deer. That lasted for a while, but we had to fish through holes in the ice to survive the rest of the winter. Luckily for us, the fish were hungry, or we would have starved. On the best of days, we set deadfalls for hares and whatever else we could get. Ever eat a weasel, Steinn? They'll help keep body and soul together, but that's about all I'll say for them."

"When the spring thaw came, we once again began our explorations. From the Scraelings, we learned about the huge lakes to the east and decided that was where we wanted to go. It wasn't easy. We had to drag the ship for short distances in places where there was no stream or sometimes around rocky rapids, but we finally made it. All the effort was worth it. We… uh…kind of persuaded some of the locals to help, if you get my drift. Those must be the biggest lakes in the world. A man could sail for months on any one of them and not see everything. We have sailed hundreds of leagues to south as well as east and there is more yet to see."

There is an empire out there, Steinn, just waiting for the right man to take it. I'd like to lead this village back there and found a city on one of the larger islands. We could have security, an endless supply of fish, wild game all around, and trees of every kind to build ships with."

"It all sounds good, Floki, but there has got to be something you are leaving out. What about your relationship with the native peoples around the lakes? It sounds to me like you might have left enemies everywhere you have been. Life is good right here and I doubt that you could persuade anyone to leave. If that is your only reason for coming here, I'm afraid you have wasted your time."

"Well, sure, that is my main purpose, and I wish you wouldn't be too hasty in making up your mind. What about the rest of the people? If some of them wanted to live on the lakes, would you refuse to let them go? You should at least let me speak to them, then they could decide for themselves. They could also have a good life there, and remember, we're all Norge. We have always been a people that lived near water, and we've always loved to sail."

"Sure, you can talk all you want, but I think I know these people better than you do. It will surprise me if you can persuade even one person to leave this compound and follow you. We have come to love the life we have here. We love to hunt the bison. We take plenty of fish from the lakes east of here. We now gather a bountiful maize crop every year. There is wild rice for the taking every fall. What more can you offer? Adventure? We don't want adventure. We want only to live in peace with the natives and to raise our families."

"Our number has grown by at least fifty souls in the last seven years. If we can maintain peace with the natives, there will come a time when we will be powerful enough that no one would dare attack us. That day is not yet, so we cannot risk upsetting the status quo. Go ahead and talk, but I am sure that what I have just said goes for all.

"We'll find out, won't we? And I have seen some of the new citizens that have been produced during my absence. Rolf's half-breeds look a lot like him, but they will never be Norge, now, will they?"

"If you would like to have your limbs torn from your body, say to Rolf what you just said to me. I'm sure he would be happy to oblige you."

After several days of using his most persuasive arguments, Floki had yet to make one convert to his cause. Some of his men were becoming so restive that he was afraid his hold on them was slipping. Maybe a bison hunt would suffice to occupy their minds until he could devise a plan to get more followers. Tomorrow morning, they would cross the river and...

"River ho!"

What now thought Steinn as he made his way to his lodge and grabbed the first weapon that he could lay hands on. We have lived here for years without one visitor, and now, we get two groups in the same week. By the time he made his way across the compound to the boat landing, several armed men were already gathered, including Floki and some of his crew. That the men in the boat were members of his own race was readily apparent from the type of clothing they wore and the color of their hair. He was excited to see strangers of his own kind in this new land. His hopes soared at the thought that there might be a village not so far away that his people could merge with.

Steinn thoroughly inspected each man from head to foot as they came ashore. He sensed no animosity from any of them as he welcomed each one separately. The apparent leader stood slightly apart from the rest of the group.

"I am called Steinn the Red for apparent reasons. I am the elected leader of this village," said stein, as he took the other man's hand in welcome.

"My name is Paul Knutson, envoy of Magnus Ericcson, king of Norway and Sweden. I have been sent to locate any survivors of the Western Greenland Settlement."

"You have found it, friend."

"Friend!" shouted Floki. Surely you can tell by his tongue, Steinn, that he is a stinking Goth. And what do you mean by king of Norway and Sweden?"

"Floki! Need I remind you that you are a guest in this village? Open your mouth once more and you will be shown the gate!" said Steinn, barely able to control his anger.

"If you will be so kind as to lend us a boat," Floki said with a sneer. "My men and I will cross the river and go bison hunting for a few days. Maybe the stench in the air will clear by the time we return. If you don't mind, I'll leave my...uh...guide here, while I'm gone."

"I apologize for the outburst Mr. Knutson. If you will come with me, we will talk while you and your men get refreshed. Normally I would be more patient, but at the present I am too much on edge to wait."

"I think I understand. Who is that man, anyway?"

"When we came to this new land, he was one of us, but he chafes at my leadership. Seven years ago, he went his own way and only recently rejoined us. He discovered some huge lakes east of here and managed, with a lot of tugging and hauling, to get his ship to them. For the last few days he has been trying to recruit followers from among the villagers to found a city on the lakes, but I am proud to say that so far, his success has been nil. One of these days I expect to have to confront him personally."

"There is nearly always someone in every group that thinks he can do a better job at leading, isn't there?"

"This is my first experience at being a leader, but I know that Floki would utterly destroy this village if he ever gained the upper hand. He is much too intolerant of anyone that isn't Norge. Ah, here comes Flora with meat and drink. If you've never tasted bison before, you're in for a treat."

Steinn fidgeted while Knutson ate. As soon as the man swallowed the last bite, he blurted: "What does the king expect from your mission?"

"King Magnus commissioned me to find out what happened to the colony on the western side of Greenland and in the process to try to bring some pagans into the Church. When I arrived in Greenland, the only living things that I found were a few ponies. I have been searching diligently for the past six years, without finding you or having much success at making converts. It is time consuming to stop at every native village, asking questions and trying to understand the answers when there is such a language barrier. I found only one village where you made contact with the natives, but many people along the coasts saw your ships. You don't know my relief now that I have found you. The king didn't give me the option of returning unsuccessful. He also wanted to be assured that you hadn't given up the True Faith."

"I can set your mind at ease in that respect. Tomorrow is Sunday and you can do us the honor of holding mass, if you wish."

"That truly would be an honor. Thank you."

"Are you supposed to try to force us to return with you to Greenland or Iceland or maybe Norway?"

"No, that is not part of my mission. I suppose that means that you and your followers are free to travel and settle where you will, but the king still looks upon you as his subjects. Forgive me for saying so, but considering the distance involved, this outpost is not worth the cost of communication. I doubt that there will ever be another effort made to contact you. My guess is that from this time on you and your people are on your own."

"That won't make anybody mad. Here, there are no taxes or exorbitant fees for religious rites. Did you know that was half the reason we left Greenland? We were little more than indentured servants to the greedy priests, and after taxes, there was little left to survive on. The burden was too grievous to bear. The other reason is because of the climate change. It became much too cold to survive."

"No, I didn't know, but I am not surprised. The farther from authority one gets, the easier it is for corruption to take hold. Greenland is a long way from Rome and Norway, too. What happened to the priests? I hope you didn't kill them before you left."

"No, of course not. When we sailed, they were standing on the beach cursing us and threatening us with excommunication, but we did them no harm. Since you found live animals, they shouldn't have starved. Maybe the Ice People killed them, or maybe the Eastern Colony rescued them. I really can't say what happened to them."

"Steinn, as far as I am concerned, my mission is over. My men and I will rest for a day, and then we will begin to gather supplies for the return trip."

"I am sorry to say that there are no accommodations for you here. Floki and his men have been camping under that large pine tree. If you wish, you can have my lodge, and I will sleep outside."

"No, no. I have been sleeping wherever I can lay my head for the past six summers. It is nothing to me to sleep on the ground. If you have an extra skin you can lend me, I would appreciate it, but otherwise I shall be fine."

"Of course, that is the least I can do."

"I would prefer to put as much space as possible between my men and Floki. There will definitely be trouble if their paths cross."

"The compound is yours to use as you wish, but Floki shouldn't be around for a few days."

"Look, Floki," said big Olaf. How much more time are we going to waste around here. Steinn has got these people under his thumb so completely that we don't stand a chance of prying any of them loose."

Floki hadn't really wanted to go bison hunting, but he had no desire to be in the vicinity of the Goths. As far as he was concerned, Goths were almost as low as Skraelings. He hated both of them with a passion.

"I know that, you idiot. What I've got to do is pry Steinn away from the people."

"And just how do you propose to do that? Steinn would make two of you, and that freak, Rolf, could tear you apart with his bare hands."

"There's a way, somehow. It just hasn't occurred to me yet. Give me time."

"That's part of my problem. I've been away from women too long already. I need some, uh, companionship. Know what I mean?"

"Yes, I know exactly what you mean. You're just like a moose in rut, and with about as much control over yourself as one, too."

"Look, Floki, I don't…"

"Shut up! Let me think for a second. You don't know it, but you might have given me an idea. Yes, I believe I know how to get Steinn to move. Listen, we'll make camp a league or two downstream to get away from the compound, and then you can go rutting. There's supposed to be a Skraeling town about 10 leagues or so farther down stream. Now you listen to me good. I want you to find a girl far enough away from the village, picking berries or whatever, that you can take without being detected. Understand?"

"Yes, of course I understand."

"I hope you do. I don't want a war party chasing you when you return. I want to be back across the river when the savages come looking for you. Now, after you capture this woman, I don't care how much you use and abuse her, but you'd better not hurt her so bad that she dies. I want her to be able to tell her story and to be able to describe in detail who it was that attacked her. Understand?"

"You're getting on my nerves, Floki. You may think I'm stupid, but I'm not. I like the plan, but I'll have to admit I don't see how this is going to get rid of Steinn."

"Well, Steinn has been trying to keep the peace with the savages around here, hasn't he? Maybe an uprising will make him want to move on, huh?"

"Yeah, maybe so. It might work. Even if it doesn't, my problem will be taken care of. When can I go?"

"The sooner the better. Let me remind you, if you get caught, you're on your own. You'll get no help from me. Do you understand that?"

"Yeah, yeah, I understand that, too. See you in a couple of days. Oh, you got any jerky you can spare? I won't have time to hunt for something to eat."

"Take what you want. The rest of us will have nothing to do but hunt while you're gone."

"Steinn," said Knutson. "I understand you have a fishing boat or two hidden on a lake not too far from here. Would it be all right if my men and I made use of it for a while? Once we start back, we won't have time to hunt and fish. If your hunters would be good enough to bring in a bison or two, we would be grateful. My men and I know nothing of bison hunting, but we are experienced fishermen."

"Yes, of course. I'm sure they would be happy to accommodate you. By the way, when you mention starting back, back to where? You can't take a rowboat back to Norway."

"No. Our ship is on the sea at the mouth of the big river. I left part of the crew there to guard it. If I don't return by the first of October, they are to assume that I am dead and are instructed to sail without me. It would be foolish to wait beyond that date."

"I will draw you a map to the lake, or if you wish I will send a man with you as a guide."

"A sketch will be enough, I am sure. If you will tell me how far to the lake and what course to hold from here, we will be on our way. Don't expect us back for at least a week."

"Well, Olaf, were you successful?" asked Floki.

"You can see that I am smiling, can't you? The savages should really be stirred up. The little wench that I abducted was a real looker. I'm sure she would have fetched a handsome bride price. I would have brought her back with me to keep for a while if you hadn't told me to let her go."

"You didn't hurt her too bad, did you?"

"No. She was fine when I let her go."

"Well, tell us all about it. We would like to hear a good story after lying around here bored for two days."

"I pulled it off without a hitch. After locating the village, I watched from the top of a nearby hill until two women left to go berry picking. Like a couple of old hens, they were making so much noise they never heard a thing as I sneaked up behind them. I clamped my left hand over the pretty one's mouth, and at the same time I gave the other one a good tap on the head with a club. She went down without a sound. It took a couple of light taps to convince my girl to cooperate, but once I had her gagged, she let me lead her like a puppy.

"You know, Floki, if you didn't hate the savages so much, we could breed our own crew. It would take a while, but a crew of half-breeds would be better than nothing at all."

"Look, if this scheme of mine works, there will be no need to consort with animals."

"Steinn will never cooperate with you under any circumstances; you should know that by now."

"If the savages attack, you can bet that Steinn will be the first one to die. Now, lets get back across the river while we can."

"Crost the river, ho! Steinn! Steinn!"

Dawn was breaking as Steinn stumbled from his lodge, wondering what the emergency could be this time. The urgency in the voice of the watchman portended trouble. "What is it, man? What's all the excitement about?"

"Look across the river, Steinn. There must be a hundred or more warriors over there, all painted up for war and armed, too."

Steinn stood dumbfounded for several seconds, not knowing what to make of the situation. By the time his reasoning returned, others were gathering around him, just as perplexed as he was.

"Falcon, what do make of this? Any idea why those warriors are gathered over there?"

"No, Steinn, I do not know. The light is not yet good, but I think they are men from my father's village. If you will permit it, I will cross the river and talk to them."

"I will go with you."

"It may not be safe. They are painted for war. I can see that much."

"It would seem cowardly of me if I didn't go. I won't take a weapon. Maybe they will be honorable enough not to kill an unarmed man."

"Yes, I think you are right. A weapon would be useless against so many, anyway. Let us go."

Falcon insisted that he row the boat alone, while Steinn sat in the bow as would be fitting for a leader. He tied the boat to a willow tree as Steinn waited. As they ascended the slope, Falcon asked Steinn to control his temper no matter what.

"Greetings my chief," said Falcon, as he quickly scanned the group of warriors. It appeared that every able-bodied man in the village was here, including his father. He gave no sign of recognition to any of the other men, giving his full attention to the chief alone.

"Am I your chief, Falcon? It has been long since you last visited the village of your birth. Maybe you are now one of the murderous pale skins? Maybe this red-haired giant is now your chief."

"This man is called Steinn. He is chief of the Norge." Turning to Steinn, he said: "This is Standing Bear, chief of my people."

"It is true that my visits are few these days, but I have taken a wife from among the Norge, and my duties as a husband keep me busy. But tell me, my chief, why do you call the Norge murderers. I know not the reason for this."

Turning to the group of warriors, Standing Bear motioned with his hand. Two middle-aged men and a young girl approached the chief. The girl had swollen lips and several bruises on her face and arms. "Do you know these people?"

"Yes, my chief. This is Rosebud, the daughter of Bison Hump, brave warrior of my people," Falcon said, indicating one of the men. And this man is Spotted Lynx, another mighty warrior of the Sisseton."

"Spotted Lynx, tell Falcon why the pale skins are called murderers."

"I once had a daughter, as you know. She was born fourteen summers ago and was ready for marriage. Now, because of a pale skinned animal, I will never hear the laughter of grandchildren."

"Bison Hump, tell Falcon what the pale skinned skunk did to your daughter."

"My daughter, Rosebud, is also fourteen summers. She, too, was ready for marriage. I say was because a pale skin savage forced himself upon her. Some of what he did to her is plain to see. Now, no suitable husband will ever be found for her. She has been sullied for life."

Falcon related everything that had been said to Steinn. "Only Floki and his men have been on this side of the river recently. Ask the girl to describe her attacker for you, Falcon."

When Rosebud had finished, Falcon turned to Steinn. "She says the man is big, with a belly like a bison cow with calf, and his body is dirty and stinking. His teeth are rotting, and his breath smells like a dead thing. There is only one man that fits that description, Steinn."

"Yes. Big Olaf. Ask the chief what he would have me do."

"Standing Bear says the murderer must pay with his own life, and since these two fathers will be denied the bride price for their daughters, someone must meet their demands."

"What! They are putting a price on their daughters? How can they think of such a thing at a time like this? I have never heard of such cold bloodied thinking before in my life."

"Steinn, among my people, daughters are considered little more than property. If the price is right, a man will sell his daughter to almost anyone. For the sake of keeping the peace, don't balk at this thing, I beg of you."

"Yes, of course. You are right. What are their demands?"

After talking to each father, Falcon translated. "They think they have you backed into a corner, Steinn. They are demanding far more than either could get under normal circumstances. They want 10 bison robes and 25 deer hides each."

"Ridiculous! There is no way that I can meet such demands. I doubt that there are that many skins in the whole village."

"I know. I believe there is another way to satisfy them. Invite the two fathers and Rosebud to the village to identify her attacker and trust me to take care of the negotiations."

"All right. What choice do I have? These are your people, and you speak the language. Invite Standing bear to come along if he will. Assure all of them that they will be perfectly safe."

The three men seemed to be nervous as they entered the boat, while Rosebud was totally unconcerned. Their vice-like grip on the seat was never relaxed until the boat bumped into the other shore. Falcon barely had room to maneuver because of the press of the three native men as the Norge men and women totally surrounded them inside the compound.

"Let me have your attention, please!" Steinn bellowed. "There has been a terrible wrong committed by one of the men in this compound. One young woman from the native village down the river has been murdered, and another one was beaten and raped."

Voices of outrage were lifted, especially among the Norge women. "What man amongst us would have done such deeds?" demanded Flora.

"This is the victim of the rape," said Steinn, indicating Rosebud. "She is here to identify the offender."

"Poor darling," chorused several female voices at once. 'Why, she's little more than a child," added another.

"Listen to me!" shouted Steinn. "I want every man in the village to line up shoulder to shoulder. Now, I want you in ranks of say twenty men to a row, with maybe two long steps between each row. I don't want any milling about that will cause confusion. Keep your place until this young lady has had a chance to look at the very last man among you. Hold it Floki! Where do you think you are off to? This goes for you and your men as well."

"Now, you listen to me, Steinn. I am fed up with your orders. You don't tell me what to do, and my men follow my command, not yours."

"What do you say about that, Rolf? Line Floki and his crew up in the next to last row and place an armed man immediately behind each one of them. If any one of them balks, bind them all hand and foot if necessary, but I want them stationary until the girl has had a good look at each one."

"Your time will come, Steinn, and believe me, you will pay dearly for the highhanded way you've treated us here this day. A man can take only so much, and you have pushed me to the limit."

"Floki, if you want to settle our differences here and now, I'm ready. If not, then shut up and get in line. If you and your men are innocent, then none of you have anything to fear."

Rosebud, along with Steinn, Falcon, and Bison Hump, went down the rows of men, looking intently at each individual, showing no sign of recognition, until she came to the fidgeting Olaf. Turning to her father she said through clinched teeth: "This is the one. Give me your knife and I will plunge it into this animal's belly."

"No, my daughter. That would be too fast a death for this man. He must die slowly and have plenty of time to think about what he has done. Would you deny Spotted Lynx the pleasure of hearing this man beg and scream until he dies?"

"I will have no personal satisfaction in such a death."

"Oh, but he will be made to run the gauntlet first. You will be placed near the end of the lines, so that when he falls you will be in a position to beat him as much as you wish, short of killing him. He then will be nursed back to health before he is burned at the stake. There will be much satisfaction for all."

"What are they saying, Falcon?" asked Steinn in a whisper. "From her actions, I would say that she has recognized Olaf."

"Yes, he is the guilty one, just as we suspected. Rosebud wants to kill him herself, but her father says that Olaf must be brought before the whole village to meet his punishment."

"What will they do to him?"

"He will pay with his life, which is fitting, but in a way that you would not want to see, I am sure."

"Olaf," said Steinn. "The girl says that you are the guilty party. You will be turned over to the natives across the river. They will take you back to their village, where you will pay for your crimes according to their system of justice. May God be merciful to you, if that is His will. You can go along peacefully, or you can be taken forcibly. The choice is yours."

"I don't have to go anywhere with anybody. Tell them Floki."

"I'm sorry Olaf. There's nothing I can do. I don't have enough men to fight this whole village."

"Now, you wait a minute, Floki. This whole thing was your idea. You wanted to start a war, so that you could kill Steinn and take his place as leader of the Norge. I'm not going to take all the blame myself. Do something, anything. You can't let them take me. Please."

"Shut up, you sniveling coward! You are the one that gave me the idea. If you weren't always like a rutting boar, maybe none of this would have taken place. You make me sick! Get him out of my sight!" said Floki, as he turned his back to walk away.

Olaf took the knife from his belt and raised it to strike Floki between the shoulder blades, but Rolf was too fast for him and wrenched the knife from his hand. Rolf wrestled Olaf to the ground, where his hands were bound behind him. The big man was helped to his feet and given a push toward the boat landing, but after two steps, he balked. It was necessary for two men, one on each arm, to half carry, half drag him-- kicking, screaming, and cursing--down to the river.

With Olaf securely in the boat, Steinn expected the three native men to get in next. When they didn't do so, Steinn turned to Falcon, "What are they waiting for?" he asked.

"The two fathers are waiting for the bride price to be settled."

"Oh, yes, I had forgotten, already. Rightfully, Floki should be the one to pay, but what has he got besides the clothes on his back?" asked Steinn.

"They all have weapons. Give me enough time to go round up an axe, a knife, a bow, whatever I can find, and we'll see what these two men think about them."

"Just in case Floki wants to resist, take five men from Rolf's squad with you."

Falcon went first to his own lodge and retrieved the shiny copper axe from its hiding place. Weeks ago, he had made a covering of beaver skin to conceal the sheen of the burnished copper, so that he could carry the axe without garnering too much attention. He next went to where Floki and crew were camping and began gathering whatever weapons he deemed most appealing to his own eyes. Floki grabbed Falcon by the left wrist and spun him around so that they were face to face. "What do you think you are doing, savage? You've no business laying hands on my possessions." Falcon's burning gaze never wavered from Floki's eyes as he calmly stated that Steinn had sent him to collect the weapons. "Would you rather these men with me take the weapons, or would you like for Steinn to come in person to get what he wants?" asked Falcon.

"That big lummox has gone way too far this time; every man has a breaking point, and I have reached mine," said Floki, his voice husky from pent up rage.

Falcon laid two each of swords, axes, bows, and hatchets before Bison Hump and Spotted Lynx. Spotted Lynx, smiling broadly, chose one of each weapon and nodded his approval, but Bison Hump, seemingly unimpressed, began a long explanation as to why the offerings were inadequate for his satisfaction.

"What is the matter, Falcon? Why does Bison Hump not even look at any of the weapons? I thought your people coveted any implement of steel."

"Yes, that is true, but this man is greedy. He says that since his daughter is still alive, and he must continue to provide for her, he should have more of a bride price than Spotted Lynx. He says that it would have been better if Rosebud had been murdered--since no man will ever want her--rather than having to spend the rest of her life as a spinster. I do not know that this would be true. Everyone seems to be able to find a mate somewhere, somehow, but to my knowledge, nothing like this has ever happened before. What are your own customs concerning such circumstances, Steinn? Is such a woman considered unclean for life in your society? How would the Norge treat Rosebud? Could you bring yourself to take such a woman as your wife?"

"In my viewpoint, Rosebud is guilty of nothing. There was no way that such a small creature could have stopped a man as big as Olaf from having his way with her. Since she was not at fault, she should have to carry no blame or shame. I don't think that ..."

"Steinn!" shouted Floki, as he forced his way between Falcon and Steinn. "This son of a she dog came to my camp and..." Without saying a word, Steinn grabbed Floki by the collar and the seat of his pants and literally threw him into the river. "Rolf, if that man opens his mouth again, use it for target practice."

"Now, Falcon, what will it take to satisfy Bison Hump?"

"He still wants the animal skins that he first demanded, as well as the weapons."

"That amounts to the price of two brides. Won't Spotted Lynx feel cheated if I give in to these demands?"

"He has stored his goods in the boat and is apparently ready to leave. I think he is quite satisfied. If Bison Hump is successful in cheating you, everyone will consider it a great joke."

"I still don't know where I can lay hands on that many hides, but I'll try to round them up, somehow. I dare not to try to please him; the price could turn out to be too high. The lives of our people cannot be measured in hides. Ask him if he will give me time to accumulate them," Steinn said, shaking his head in despair."

"Steinn, take this copper axe," said Falcon, as he covertly slipped the copper axe to Steinn, "and when I tell you, take the cover from it and slowly turn it so that the sunlight will reflect off it."

"Falcon. This axe is your most valued possession. You spent many, many days working it to perfection. I can't accept such a sacrifice from you. Somehow, I will come up with the hides."

"Starting tomorrow, I will begin another axe. If you wish, you can assist me. Now, allow me to play a little with Bison Hump's mind. He must be made to desire the axe above all things."

"Bison Hump is a wise man to spurn such common weapons such as these lying here on the ground. I happen to know that Steinn, as chief of the Norge, has a most uncommon weapon. It is such a beautiful and unusual weapon that only a mighty warrior should own it. The warrior lucky enough to own this precious, one-of-a-kind object would soon be known throughout the forests to the east and the plains to the west. He would have the envy of every warrior of every tribe. You have this man at your mercy. To prevent war, he can be persuaded to relinquish this weapon."

Bison Hump's curiosity was certainly piqued. "You have done a lot of talking. Show this weapon to me that I may decide for myself how valuable it is."

"First, I must tell you that this object is so valuable that nothing additional will be offered. You must accept the original offer of the iron weapons and hides, or this object by itself, but there is a hitch, Steinn will not give this weapon to you as a bride price unless he receives something in return."

"How can he make any demands at all? I have seen nothing of value except the iron weapons, not even one animal skin. What does he want from me?"

"If he pays the price for a bride, he must have the bride. You will have to relinquish your daughter to him as his bride. Do you agree to this?

"How can I say yes or no? My patience is at an end. Now, show this valuable object to me without further delay, or I shall end all discussion."

Falcon nodded to Steinn that the time was right to reveal the copper axe. "Thrust the axe close to Bison Humps face in such a way that he will see the handle first, then make a ceremony of taking the cover off. His anticipation must be heightened to the utmost."

When Steinn pointed the axe handle in Bison Hump's direction, the man actually took a step backward. The carving was so realistic that the effect was that of a live snake about to strike. As Steinn slowly removed the beaver skin covering, Bison Hump inched closer, bending forward for a better look and rubbing his sweating palms on his leggings.

Steinn slowly drew the covering aside until only a glimmer of burnished copper was revealed, then paused. Bison Hump glanced up at Steinn's face, and then looked at Falcon in wonderment. When he looked again at the axe, Steinn removed the beaver skin with a flourish. As Steinn slowly turned the axe to catch the sunlight, Bison Hump stood agog, with fingers twitching in anticipation of touching the most beautiful object he had ever seen.

"Can you imagine owning such a sacred object, Bison Hump?" asked Falcon, trying to add value to the axe by presenting it as a ceremonial object.

"It is truly beautiful, the most glorious creation I have ever seen."

"A man could not offer enough animal skins to buy this precious axe, since there is no other like it upon the earth, only for the sake of keeping peace between our peoples, will Steinn relinquish ownership of it. Will you accept it as the bride price for your daughter?"

"Yes, it is enough. I will proudly possess this axe," said Bison Hump, as he extended both hands, palms up, as if to receive a newborn baby. "From this day forward!" he cried, as he triumphantly held the axe above his head, "My name shall be Red Axe. I will carry this axe always in battle. I can feel its power flowing into my body at this very moment. With this axe in my hand, I will be invincible. The enemy will quake at the mention of my name."

Standing Bear and Spotted Lynx had come ashore and made their way to stand in awe before Bison Hump. Falcon hoped that all negotiations would be completed before jealousy became a factor.

"Daughter, you have heard what has transpired. You are to become this man's wife. I could never expect to do any better for you. He is the chief of this village; you will be the wife of a chief. I expect you to act with the dignity worthy of such a position."

"Are you going to tell me what is going on?" Steinn asked Falcon.

"Everything is falling into place. Bison Hump will accept the axe under one condition. You must take Rosebud as your bride. Now that the price of a bride has been met, she is yours."

"Whoa, now! Let's back up a little. Earlier he was saying that he would have to provide for her the rest of her life. Why the sudden change?"

"Earlier he was using Rosebud for the purpose of take advantage of you. Now that the hides are no longer a factor in the deal, she has become a liability. Most fathers look forward to the day when they can marry off their daughters. There is one fewer mouth to feed, and of course there is the bride price to consider. He is getting rid of a daughter and gaining something of value. He is satisfied."

"He may be satisfied, but I am not. When I decide to marry, it will be with a woman of my own choosing."

Steinn, this matter is practically settled. Do you want to destroy all that has been gained? You shouldn't be too hasty in your refusal. Taking this girl would be a small price to pay to keep your people safe. Do you find her unattractive? Is she not good enough for you, since she has been…uh… soiled?"

"It's not that, Falcon. She's a lovely girl, one of the best looking I've ever seen, and I've already told you that she is not unclean in my opinion, but she is a total stranger to me. I have no feelings for her."

"Love will come in its own good time, Steinn. Right now, peace should be your main concern."

Yes, of course, you are right. I must learn to think before I act. My people must always come first. Tell Bison Hump it is agreed. It looks as if I'll be a married man before sundown. Blessed Mary please help me."

"Steinn, it won't be so bad, I guarantee it," said Falcon. He could hardly contain his glee as he turned toward Bison hump to clinch the deal. Rosebud, having stood quietly throughout the proceedings, had heard everything that had been said, and now accepted that she was to be the wife of the red-haired giant. She knew that she would never return to her village, nor would she get to see her abductor punished for his crimes. These strange people with such a strange tongue would now become her people. Could she ever bear it? Or would it be better to steal a knife and kill herself? No, she would never shame her father and family in such a way.

The native men and Falcon returned to the boat to cross to the other side of the river as Steinn, Rolf, and the squad, after picking up the weapons, walked back toward the center of the village. Rolf's chosen group of twenty young men as his most trusted friends, men who were willing to take orders from him unquestioningly, acted as an unofficial police force. He had also, with Steinn's approval, assumed the leadership position of this squad, as it was now called. Since the arrival of Floki such an outfit was needed as never before.

Rosebud stood alone, not knowing what to do or where to go, until Helga and Flora came to her aid. They didn't know that Rosebud was to become Steinn's wife, since they knew nothing of the negotiations, but she was alone, and that was enough to make them want to help her. They couldn't communicate with the young woman, but they tried by being friendly to make her feel welcome.

Steinn, with Rolf and the squad, went straight to Floki's camp. Floki was still dripping from his dunk in the river. The dousing had done nothing to cool his anger, maybe even having the opposite effect, as the fire of hatred in his eyes was plain to see.

"Floki, you and your men have five minutes to gather your belongings and be through that gate, or I swear that all of you will be cut down where you stand. The only weapons you will be allowed to take with you are your daggers. Now, get moving."

"How far do you think we'd get without weapons? You are sentencing us to death, Steinn."

"It is better than you deserve. I should kill you myself right now. How many people would have died if your scheme had been successful? You now have four minutes."

"Let's go, Floki," several of his nervous followers said at once.

"Where is Raven Wing?" asked Floki.

Raven Wing stepped from behind Steinn, where he had been hiding. "Raven Wing not go."

"Yes, you're going. You came here with me; you're leaving with me. Now come on."

"Raven Wing not go."

Floki took a step toward the young man, intending to seize him. "Back off Floki," said Steinn. "He plainly said that he doesn't want to go with you. Leave him be."

"For Christ's sake, Floki, let's go. We should never have come here to begin with. Everything has gone wrong. We're worse off now than we've ever been."

A young blond-haired man, who had been slowly sidestepping to put some distance between Floki and himself, spoke up. "Steinn, if you will allow it, I'd like to stay, too. I don't want to follow Floki any more. I'll do anything you say, if you will let me join you."

"All right, but to be trusted, you will have to prove yourself first. You understand that don't you?"

"Yes. After all that has taken place, I expected nothing else."

"What is your name?"

"Eric Orvalson."

"Eric, You traitor! You yellow dog!" shouted Floki, spouting words of hatred over his shoulder as he stormed toward the gate. "If I ever see you again, I will skin you alive. I mean it; I will literally skin you alive. I will carve the flesh from your body a sliver at a time. You will beg me to slit your throat before you die."

"Falcon, would you take Pall and follow Floki's trail, at a safe distance mind you, to make sure he doesn't hang around here. I wouldn't allow him weapons because I want anyone who may venture outside the wall to be safe, but I still don't trust him. Give him a good head start, then follow him for at least 10 leagues to make sure he's left the area."

"Well, everybody, this has been a very trying day for me. I think I could go for a cup of wine, a bite to eat, and a nap. Do I have any takers on that idea?"

"Uh, Steinn, are we going to get to attend a wedding today?" asked Rolf.

"Aaaaagh!" Growled Steinn, through clenched teeth. "You just had to remind me, didn't you? I was hoping that part of the deal could somehow be avoided, but I don't see any way around it. A bargain is a bargain. I'll uphold my end of it. May it never be said that Steinn reneged on a deal."

Rolf seemed as pleased as Falcon at the prospect of Steinn taking a wife.

"Rolf, if you would, assemble everyone at the river. We'd might as well get this thing over with. Where did the girl get off to, anyway?

"Don't worry, Steinn. I'll find her. She couldn't have gone far."

When all the people were gathered near the river, Steinn related to them the details of the negotiations with the natives. He told them again how Olaf had killed one girl and abducted and raped another. Their anger was kindled anew at Olaf's crime, but the anger turned to outrage when Floki's evil plan was revealed. Glee replaced all feelings of anger and outrage at Steinn's final revelation: in order to preserve the peace, they had enjoyed for years, it would be necessary to take Rosebud as his wife. Her father had insisted that since Steinn had paid the bride price, the marriage must take place.

"Now don't look at this thing as punishment, Steinn," said Flora. "Just like every other man, you need a woman to take care of you." Steinn only frowned amidst the gales of laughter, especially from the women. They considered his dejected look a great joke.

With the whole village watching, Steinn took the hand of Rosebud and led her into the river. Since falcon and Pall, the only two people who could speak the Sisseton language, were absent, Rosebud had no definite idea about what was taking place. Whatever it was, she would accept it as stoically as any male warrior of her tribe. If Steinn meant to drown her, so be it. Death may be preferable to being an outcast stuck in this village of strange people. She had heard her father say that the ordeal with Olaf had made her unclean--she didn't feel unclean—but maybe the red-haired giant would rather drown her than to marry her as he had promised.

The words that Steinn was saying had no meaning for her. As he covered her nose with his hand, she did not protest. She was calm as he laid her backward into the river. Her body was completely submerged in the water, but she felt no fear. She was puzzled, when after only a moment under the water she was raised again. As Steinn led her back to the bank, her wonderment was complete, when she saw the two kind women who had attended her earlier crying and smiling at the same time. They each hugged her tightly in turn and mumbled something unintelligible in her ear. Maybe that dunking in the river was these people's way of making her clean again. So be it.

"Rolf, now that Rosebud has had a Christian baptism, would you perform the marriage ceremony for us, please?"

"Steinn, I'm not a priest. I don't know anything about marrying people. The only ceremony I remember is the one you performed for Helga and me. Would that be sufficient?"

"That would be fine. You're just as married as anybody can possibly be, aren't you?"

"Well, Helga says so. Has anybody got a piece of string?" Someone produced a piece of rawhide and handed it to Rolf. After tying the couple's fingers together, Rolf said: "Before God and all the witnesses standing here, I now pronounce you man and wife. Uh, you may kiss the bride, Steinn."

Steinn gave his bride a perfunctory hug but didn't even attempt to kiss her.

All Steinn could do was stand and grin sheepishly as the men formed a line to shake his hand and congratulate him on his marriage. Rosebud was still puzzled about what had taken place, as the women hugged her and welcomed her as a new member of the village. She didn't know what she had done to receive so much praise, but she was glad she had done it. She felt surprisingly good about all the attention being lavished upon her. Maybe this was a foretaste of her new status as the wife of a chief.

After Steinn had led her to his lodge, Rosebud began to realize that the ceremony she had gone through must have been a marriage ceremony. How she wished Falcon could be here to explain everything to her. How could she ever function when she understood not one word of this strange language? What was she to do? Her husband had brought her to this place, said something incomprehensible, and left. Now, dusk was falling and there was not even enough light to explore the interior of the lodge. All she could do was sit on the floor and wait.

She decided then and there to remain inside the lodge forever and become as invisible as possible, but no sooner had she made this resolution than the Norge woman that looked so much like one of her own kind arrived. Rosebud followed as the woman took her hand and led the way to another lodge. Several people, including the pale woman that had been so friendly earlier, were gathered around an outside cooking fire. Steinn was there, too, but he acted as if he had never seen her before. Well, what was she to expect? Even though they were man and wife, they were strangers, with no means of communication.

Rosebud smelled the aroma of boiling stew and realized that she was famished. She had eaten nothing since early morning, but the day had been too eventful to think of food. Now, if only someone would give her a bowl of the stew, she would eat it, no matter whether it was well cooked or not.

As she took a seat beside a pretty red-haired woman, the people around her were laughing and talking just like her own people would be doing at the evening meal at home. At home, she thought. How easy it was to forget that this was her home, now. That thought made her want to cry. If only she knew the language, maybe she wouldn't feel so self conscious and alone. Oh, Falcon where are you, she wondered.

The stew was delicious, even though it had a slightly different flavor than she was used to. Maybe the big iron pot that it was cooked in made the difference. There had been no heated rocks dropped into the stew to boil it. Rosebud had never seen anything like the pot before. Obviously, the fire over which it was suspended had no effect on it. One couldn't do that with a cooking skin.

When the meal was finished, it seemed that no one but Rosebud was anxious to leave. It was the middle of September and as the night progressed a slight breeze gave the air a chill, but the heat from the fire lulled her into drowsiness. She wanted nothing more than to curl up in a fetal position and go to sleep, never to awaken. Finally, after what seemed like hours to Rosebud, Steinn took her hand and led the way between the other lodges back to his own home. Knowing what might take place once inside the lodge, made her heart beat faster, from fear as well as a certain reluctant excitement.

Steinn led her to the sleeping mat and lay down beside her fully clothed. Rosebud waited several minutes to see what Steinn would do before she pulled the cover up to her chest and fell into a deep sleep.

Shortly after dawn, Steinn arose, and after breaking the fast with rice cakes and cold bison meat, began to sharpen and clean the rust from weapons that had been long neglected by Floki and crew. As he worked, his hands moved automatically, but his mind was elsewhere. There was only one thought on his mind: the young woman only a few away that had become his wife. It still didn't seem real, yet he knew it was. He didn't want a wife, but there was no honorable way to get rid of her.

Then he had a thought that made him drop the sword he was working on! What if Rosebud were pregnant? How could he ever accept a child that belonged to that stinking pig Olaf? He had tried to be magnanimous in telling Falcon that being raped had not defiled the girl, but he had been a hypocrite. It did make a difference. Half his objection to being married would disappear if the girl were a virgin. He knew in his heart that he had to overcome such thinking if he were ever to keep the respect of his people. He closed his eyes and silently prayed for help in handling this problem.

Steinn picked up the sword and began scouring the rust from the blade as Helga arrived to ask for Rosebud. "She is still inside, but I believe she is awake. I've heard movement."

"Steinn, would it be all right if Rosebud stayed with me the rest of the day?" Helga asked. "I'll try to teach her a few words of our language each day. The sooner she can communicate, the sooner she will fit in. Don't you agree?"

"Yes, of course. The sooner the better. I will be indebted to you."

"Nonsense. I can still remember how I felt. If Rolf had been less patient, I would have hurt a lot more. And believe me, Steinn, it does hurt to be cut off from everything you have ever known and thrust into a strange new world. But look at me now; I am just as much Norge as you are. Give Rosebud a few weeks, and you will see a big difference in her. Wait and see."

Steinn already felt relieved, simply because Rosebud would have someone to keep company with. Rolf was obviously a much better man than he was in some respects; he had shown much devotion to Helga from the very beginning. Rosebud, on the other hand, might as well be alone, as to be with him. This way he could attend to his own business without worrying about her. If she wanted, she could live with Rolf and Helga forever. That would be the perfect solution to his problem. He smiled at the thought.

VIII

"Floki," said Karl Herjolfson, Floki's new lieutenant, the best choice to replace big Olaf. "We need to talk. We can't charge headlong through this wilderness with no weapons except daggers. Get the hate for Steinn out of your mind, so that you can think. We've got to come up with something. I've got an idea if you're interested in listening."

"Alright men, let's rest for a minute. What have you got on your mind, Karl?"

"Have you noticed that we are following the trail made by Knutson and his men?"

"No, Karl. You said it right. My hate for Steinn has had me blinded. I want to carve him up so bad that I can't think of anything else. But now that you've got my attention, I think I get your drift. Knutson has weapons. If we use our heads, we can get those weapons for ourselves."

"Yes, you catch on fast; that is my very thought."

"All right, I need one man to go on ahead and locate Knutson's camp, then double back along the trail to intercept us. We need to know the layout of their camp; how many men are in it;

how many are out in the boats; and anything else that might be important. Nils, I believe you are the best tracker of this group; I'm going to trust you with this mission. Think you can handle it?"

"Sure, Floki, I don't foresee any problem."

"Well, get along then, and don't let anybody see you. Intercept us on the trail about a league from their camp, and we'll plan our strategy before making our move."

When the group came to the south fork of the Bison River, Floki decided to spend the night there. They had no food, but at least they would have all the water they could drink. None of the men knew anything about living off the land. Some of them wanted to try eating the roots of plants growing nearby, but Floki told them that this was no time to take the chance of becoming sick. He would need every man in good physical condition when they located Knutson's camp. They had missed a few meals before and suffered no permanent damage. He wanted to hear no more griping.

With the coming of dawn, Floki had the men moving. He could hear several voices of low grumbling but decided to tolerate the protestations as long as they didn't get out of hand. When their bellies were full again, everything would be right with the world.

According to the position of the sun, it was mid afternoon when Nils stepped from behind a tree into the trail only a few feet ahead of Floki. Without thinking, Floki went into a crouched, and his hand automatically went to his dagger. "Nils, you idiot. Lucky for you I didn't have a halberd in my hand. Couldn't you have simply been standing in the trail?"

"Sorry, Floki. Didn't know you were so nervous."

"Well, what did you find out?"

"I found the camp without any trouble at all. I watched them for a couple of hours, maybe more. There are 10 men on shore tending to the drying racks. Some are chopping wood, some are stoking the fires, and others are cleaning fish. The men in the boats bring in the catch periodically, and then go back out. Just about what you would expect in this kind of camp."

"Now listen to me and listen good. To carry out my plan without anybody getting hurt, each one of you will have to do his part without hesitation and without making any mistakes. Now, here is what we will do…"

Pall returned to the village just as dusk was falling. The young man was tired, footsore, hungry, and thirsty. He had come from the Lake of the Cormorants in record time, not stopping for anything except to drink from the south fork of the Bison River in the early afternoon. But before taking care of his personal needs, he must talk to Steinn.

"Steinn could see immediately from Pall's bedraggled condition that something important was in the air. "Pall, where is Falcon? Is he all right?"

"It's not Falcon, Steinn. He's fine. Could I have a drink, while I catch my breath."

"I'm sorry, Pall. I wasn't thinking."

After Pall had slaked his thirst, he took a deep breath and began to relate what had taken place over the past two and a half days. "Steinn, a terrible thing has taken place. A thing so horrible

I don't want to close my eyes, because every time I do, I see the horror of it all over again, in every gory detail."

"Falcon and I gave Floki and crew a good head-start before we began following them. We figured correctly that they would camp at the river ford, so we crossed the river down stream and made our way up the other side until we could see their campfire, then we backed off to a safe distance and made our own camp, which was really nothing but a place to sleep. The next morning, we watched as they crossed the river, then we gave them an hour's head start."

"Late in the afternoon we came in sight of the lake. Falcon asked me to stay concealed while he reconnoitered. When he came back about an hour later, I could tell that something was very wrong. All he said to me was: 'Come.'"

"Before we got completely inside the camping area, I could see bodies scattered about, all covered with blood. I didn't get real close to them, but I could see that some had been stabbed, while others had their throats cut. None of the dead were Floki's men, but Falcon said from blood in the trail that led from the campsite along the western shore of the lake that at least one of the killers was wounded, though he couldn't tell how badly. It was the worst thing I have ever seen, Steinn. I don't know if I will ever get it out of my mind."

Steinn, had listened to the gruesome story without comment, and even now could find nothing to say. He could do nothing except shake his head, his face as pale as a ghost. If he hadn't been so soft hearted toward Floki, this wouldn't have happened. Why were there such cruel and selfish men in the world?

"Was Knutson among the dead, Pall?"

"I…didn't make a close examination of the bodies, Steinn, but I don't think he was one of them."

"I'm going to get Rolf and the squad. You can remain behind and help take care of the village if you want to. It looks like you could use some rest. We'll be gone as soon as it is light enough to see. I don't know when we will be back. I really don't know what we're up against."

"Steinn, I'm part of the squad. I'll get my mother to pack a bag for me, and after I get some rest, I'll be ready to go with you."

"Do you think you can hold up? We won't slow down for you. If you can't keep up, we'll have to leave you behind."

"I know. I wouldn't expect you to do otherwise."

"Well, then, fill your belly and get a few hours sleep. We leave at first light."

Steinn was proud of the young man. He had come a long way toward maturity since the first bison hunt.

Steinn related to Rolf and the others the grisly story. The reaction was about what he expected. If Floki could be captured right now, he would certainly be put to the sword. No one seemed to lay any blame for what had happened on Steinn. Everyone believed that banishing Floki and crew with nothing but daggers amounted to a death sentence, but from the looks of things, Floki had been grossly underestimated.

Steinn told the men to pack enough food for three days. He wanted at least half of the squad to be armed with bows and plenty of arrows. If a fight ensued, he hoped it could be fought at a distance. It worried him that some of his friends could be harmed or killed.

Almost as an afterthought, Steinn asked Helga if she would look after Rosebud while he was gone, and if there was any way possible, to please explain to her what was going on. It was easy for him to forget about Rosebud. He still had a hard time thinking of the girl as his wife, and his responsibility.

The men left the compound at a fast walk, a pace that would be held until their journey was almost completed. They followed the Bison River to its southernmost point then struck out across country toward Cormorant Lake. Darkness fell an hour before the group reached their destination, but an early rising moon made it possible to continue on at a much slower pace. They didn't need a trail to follow, since all of them had been to the lake before on fishing trips.

Falcon was sitting beside the trail awaiting their arrival. It would be best, he explained, to camp where they were rather than getting any closer to the murder site. The bodies, having lain in the sun for so long, were beginning to putrefy. None of the tired trekkers wanted to go farther in the darkness anyway. All they wanted was a bite to eat and a good night of rest.

The next morning, Falcon, advised the men not to eat anything unless they had a very strong composition. The sight of the bodies combined with the stench would surely upset some stomachs. None of the men seemed anxious to go to the murder site, but it must be done. The bodies deserved a decent burial; it was the least they could do.

A flock of crows and vultures arose from the bodies as the group of men approached. The birds had been at the bodies for some time; flies were amassed at mouths, noses, wounds, and empty eye sockets. It wasn't a pretty sight. Falcon, having become inured to the condition of the bodies, was the only man that did not get sick. Three men of the group became so helpless from continual retching that they were relieved of their duties and sent away from the site until burial was completed. The ones with strong enough constitutions to do the job were asked to drag the bodies and place them side-by-side in a row.

A single shovel was found among the scattered tools left behind. Sand from the lakeshore was shoveled into whatever container that could be found, some of the men using their shirts, and carried to the bodies. Others began carrying stones from along the shore of the lake to be placed over the mass grave to keep animals away from the bodies. After three hours of hard labor, Steinn said he was satisfied with their efforts. There was nothing more they could do for the dead men. He repeated as best he could the words remembered from other burials he had attended. Maybe Knutson would want to perform his own burial rites later, that is, if he could be found.

As the men who had touched the bodies stripped to bathe in the lake, Steinn found a shady place to sit, while Falcon related what he believed had taken place. "I have been over the whole area, even all the way around the lake, since Pall left to get you. What I have deducted from the evidence is that Floki and his nine men were allowed into this camp, probably on the pretence of friendship. Being unarmed, except for daggers, they would not have seemed much of a threat to Knutson's men. Being equal in number, each of Floki's men would have chosen his target. At a prearranged signal from Floki, they would have struck simultaneously, giving the victims no chance to defend themselves."

Steinn made no comment, merely nodding his head in agreement.

"I found the trail made by the killers as they left this area, probably taking the dead men's weapons and carrying as much dried fish as possible. They went north along the lakeshore before turning east. Having found no evidence of Knutson or the fishing boats, I left Floki's trail and started southward around the lake. Not until I reached the southern most point of the lake did I find where Knutson had come ashore. His trail pointed directly southward for as far as I followed it. He made no attempt at stealth. I believe his only thought was to distance himself from this area as quickly as possible. The trail should be easy enough to follow."

"Good work, Falcon. I'm sure that Knutson is no more of a woodsman than I am. He probably left a trail that a blind man could follow, but you have saved us a lot of time by having it all figured out. We have time to cover a few leagues before dark. Ill get everyone ready, and we'll be off. We'll take the few bags of dried fish that Floki left behind. That will extend our meager rations a little farther."

Instead of going east to the place where Knutson came ashore, Falcon led the group in a southerly direction, hoping to save time by intercepting the trail as far to the south as possible. Before they had gone three leagues, a lake barred the way. No sign of a trail had yet been seen, which meant that Knutson must have skirted the lake toward the eastern side. Falcon headed eastward along the northern shore of the lake, and shortly found the trail they had been seeking. After passing the eastern end of the lake, the trail led south once more. The track skirted two more lakes close together.

Dusk was falling when the group neared the end of the third body of water, causing Steinn to call an immediate halt to give the men time to eat and prepare a place to sleep, if they so desired. A good night of rest would be welcomed by all of them, especially Pall, who, even though worn to a frazzle, had worked as hard as anyone throughout the day.

As some of the men gathered firewood, Steinn moved several yards distance from the main group to find a suitable place to make his bed. Even though all the men were tired, they couldn't seem to put the horrid details of the day out of their minds. Steinn heard several comments about what should be done to Floki if he were ever caught. Some of the suggestions were as barbarous as the acts Floki himself had committed.

It wasn't long before Falcon lay down not far from Steinn. Both men were soon asleep, but the nights were getting quite cool this time of year, and with a breeze blowing from across the lake, Steinn awoke some time later with a chill. The discussion among the other men having ended, Steinn moved closer to the campfire to spend the rest of the night. Falcon, on the other hand, seemingly impervious to the cold, remained where he was.

After a hasty breakfast, the group was on the trail again as soon as the gathering light allowed. Falcon, leading the way, followed the trail unerringly. Steinn, second in line, thought that even he could follow such plain spoor as this. A dozen bison traveling in single file would have left tracks hardly more conspicuous than these men had made.

The pace that had been set was somewhat slower than the day before, making another night of camping necessary. Steinn figured they had traveled about twenty leagues since leaving the murder scene. Just how far would Knutson go, anyway? And why was he going south?

If Knutson weren't found soon, some hunting would be necessary to augment the food supply. The men were already getting tired of fish and rice cakes. Tomorrow he would let some of the men try for a deer.

Before noon of the next day, after traversing a long stretch with no lakes, Falcon called a halt near a shallow body of water with a small island in it. He showed Steinn where the trail ended with footprints in the mud at the shoreline. If everyone would stay where they were, he would scan the area to see if another trail led away from the area. After making a quick survey along the lakeshore without finding more sign, Falcon informed Steinn that Knutson must be on the island.

"Knutson! Paul Knutson! Are you there, Knutson?" Steinn yelled, at the top of his voice.

After what seemed the better part of a minute, a head peered from around a tree on the island. Paul Knutson stepped into the open, a bow with knocked arrow ready. "Steinn? I sure am happy to see you. Is it safe to cross over? There's none of Floki's men with you, is there?"

"No, Paul, they have left the area. From the evidence we've found, they have gone east toward the great lake, back to where they left the ship. But how did you know for sure it was Floki that killed your men?"

Before Knutson could answer, his men, who had been listening to the conversation, burst from the trees and began to slosh through the waist deep channel, laughing and yelling from sheer relief. They had been living in fear of their lives since finding the slain men at the fishing camp. With a release of tension came a flood of tears from some of the men. They wept unashamedly; there was no resemblance between these men and the fierce plunderers that were their ancestors of four centuries ago.

"Now, to answer your question, Steinn. There was no other logical conclusion that we could come to. We examined the bodies close enough to see that the wounds weren't made with stone knives, and Floki, as I am sure you remember, was spewing so much venom the day we arrived at your village that we figured it had to be him. None of the natives we have encountered over the years ever demonstrated so much hatred toward us. I don't know why those men have so much spite in their hearts, but only hate can make a man mutilate a dead body. Not only were their throats cut, they were stabbed and slashed multiple times, but I suppose you have already been to the murder scene, otherwise, you wouldn't be here."

"Yes, we've already buried the bodies, but it was difficult to determine the full extent of the wounds. Vultures had done extensive damage to them."

"Paul, I can understand why you were in such a hurry to get away from the murder site, but why you came to this place is what I can't figure out. My village is actually closer. Why didn't you come that way?"

"Yes, I know the distances involved. We intended to leave this island camp first thing tomorrow morning and make our way west to the Red River, and then north along the river to your compound, but I had a project to finish on the island first. As to the reason we came here: if you consider our predicament after we found the bodies, you might have done the same thing, I am sure. Since we were on the lake out of sight of the fishing camp, we had no idea where the killers had gone after they had done their deed. They could have been waiting nearby for us to flee toward your village, that being the obvious escape route; therefore, we couldn't go west. We knew that Floki had left his ship on the great eastern lake. To make his way east, he would naturally go north around the lake before turning eastward, so to flee north or east would also be dangerous. Though we outnumbered them, a fight was out of the question. After taking most of our weapons, they would be well armed, while we had taken only a few knives and one bow with us in the fishing boats. The only option, to my thinking, was to escape to the south with all haste. We came all this way before finding a place that was defensible. Even if they followed us this far, we could make it too costly for them to try to cross to the island."

"I can see your reasoning; it's quite logical, once you think about it. Do you want to take the project you mentioned with you when you leave?"

"No. If I had known that we would survive this ordeal, I wouldn't have bothered with it in the first place, but in case we were all killed, I chiseled a message into a slab of stone to tell anyone that might come searching for us what had happened. There was only a slight chance that the stone would ever be found, but I had to do something."

"Have you had much to eat the last few days?"

"Our best bowman brought in a few geese and ducks and one beaver. We could eat if you have anything to spare."

"Take what you want. I have four men out hunting; hopefully, one of them will bring in a deer. One deer won't go far with this many men; we'll have to do more hunting."

After the men had eaten, Steinn asked to see the stone with the message on it. He and Knutson waded across the shallow strait to the island. The stone had been sunk into the soil far enough to hold it upright. Steinn, as he knelt to read the inscription, thought the stone looked way too much like a grave marker. He hoped it wasn't an ill omen.

8:GOTHS:AND:22:NORRMEN:ON:EXPLORA-TION:JOURNEY:FROM:

VINLAND:WESTWARD:WE:HAD:-CAMP:BY:2:ROCKY:ISLETS:ONE:

DAYS:JOURNEY:NORTH:FROM:THIS:-STONE:WE:FISHED:A:DAY:

AFTER:WE:CAME:HOME:FOUND:10:MEN:RED:WITH:BLOOD:AND:

DEAD: A V' M:SAVE:FROM:EVIL

Down the narrow-left side, a further inscription had been made.

HAVE:10:MEN:BY:THE:SEA:

TO:LOOK:AFTER:OUR:SHIP:

14:DAYS:JOURNEY:FROM:

THIS:ISLAND:YEAR:1362

Steinn got to his feet and turned toward Knutson. "Hopefully, Paul, no one will need to read this. What do you intend to do now? Do you want to go back to the lake or to the village?"

"I want to visit the grave of my men first, and then I must go after Floki. I cannot leave this land without knowing that he has paid the ultimate price for his crimes."

"If you go after Floki, there is no way you will be able to make the trip back to your ship before the first of October. You will be left behind for sure. Are you willing to spend the rest of your life in this land?"

"My men and I have discussed this very thing over and over. We all agree that we cannot walk away and ignore what Floki has done. Our consciences will not permit such action, and besides the king would surely be angry with us. You and the others came to this land to make it your home. I can do the same? If you will allow it, my men and I will become part of your village. Here, read this," said Knutson, as he handed Steinn a folded paper from inside his shirt.

Steinn, after removing the protective cover, unfolded the paper and began to read aloud:

"Magnus, by the Grace of God king of Norway, Sweden and Skaane, sends to all men who see or hear this letter good health and happiness. We desire to make known that you, Paul Knutson, are to take the men who are to go in the Knorr whether they be named or not named, from my bodyguard and also from among the retainers of other men whom you may wish to take on the voyage, and that Paul Knutson, who shall be the commandant upon the Knorr, shall have full authority to select the men who are best suited either as officers or men. We ask you to accept this, our command, with a right good will for the cause, inasmuch as we do it for the honor of God and for the sake of our soul, and for the sake of our predecessors, who in Greenland established Christianity and have maintained it to this time, and we will not let it perish in our days. Know this for truth, that whoever defiles this, our command, shall meet with serious displeasure and thereupon receive full punishment."

"Executed at Bergen, Monday after Simon and Judah's day in the six and XXX year of our reign (1354). By Orm Ostenson, our regent, sealed."

"So, you see, Steinn, by attacking my men, Floki attacked the king. There is no way that I can face the king without knowing that Floki has been punished to the utmost. If I had only had the weapons needed, I should have been on his trail all this time."

"Let's go back to the men; I have a story to tell you concerning Floki."

When the two men came back to the camp, the hunters had returned and had two deer hanging from nearby trees. Fresh liver, kidneys, and strips of meat were roasting over the fire. Steinn waited until everyone was sated before beginning the story of how Floki had brought the Norge to the brink of war. For the next half hour, Knutson and crew sat spellbound, listening to every detail of the story.

"So, you see, by handing Olaf over to the Sisseton, meeting the bride prices, and agreeing to marry the daughter of Bison Hump, we barely escaped the threat of war with the seven allied tribes. To have his way, Floki was willing to risk the lives of everyone, including women and children. I wanted him to have plenty of time to think about his crimes while he was struggling to live in the wilderness, but by banishing him from the village without weapons, I probably doomed those poor men to death. I have to go with you to find Floki to expiate my guilt. Like you, I have to know that he is dead before I can have peace of mind."

"I will welcome your company, but don't blame yourself for what happened. I should think that under ordinary circumstances that a slow death from starvation would be the result of such a sentence. How could you have known what would happen? Floki is a sick and dangerous man. He must be destroyed the same as a rabid dog."

"Oh, by the way, congratulations on your marriage," Knutson said with a wide grin, while Falcon looked at the ground to hide his own smile.

"We'll have to take Raven Wing with us. I wouldn't want to approach any native village with this many armed men, especially since Floki has preceded us," said Steinn. "He has a knack for making enemies wherever he goes. We won't need all these men. Some of them can return to the village, and one of them can bring back Raven Wing and the weapons that I confiscated from Floki."

"Rolf, I hate to do this to you; I know that you and the others would like to take part in the hunt, but we just don't need so many men. There will still be Knutson with 11 men, Falcon, the man you send back with Raven Wing, and myself. That is 16 men to provide for, way too many, but I don't want to deprive any of Knutson's group of the opportunity to hunt down the killers. You can head northwest from here, and the rest of us will go directly north. We will meet the man of your choosing and Raven Wing at the massacre site."

After much grumbling, the squad left for home. Only Rolf would return with Raven Wing and as many weapons as the two of them could carry.

Knutson held his own burial ceremony at the mass grave. All his men had friends among the dead and would love to get their hands on the killers. Steinn wondered if Floki would be given a chance to surrender if caught, or would he simply be cut down without ceremony. Whatever punishment was meted to him would not be sufficient to pay for his crimes.

Steinn and some of the other men spent two days hunting while waiting for Rolf. When the heavily laden Rolf and Raven

Wing arrived, Knutson's men were anxious to get on the trail, but since the day was already far gone, Steinn wanted to give the two tired men a chance to rest before starting the chase. The majority of the men being of Knutson's party, Steinn asked him to lead the group, but Knutson declined on the grounds that he and his men from this day forward would be guests in Steinn's village.

Early the next morning, the group of men got under way. Raven Wing estimated it would take a week, hunting for food as they went, to reach his village on the great lake. The course he set as they left the murder site was as close to directly east as the various trails permitted, but he told Steinn that they would probably have to make several detours because of lakes, Lakota villages, and a range of steep hills that lay in their path. There being no single path leading directly east to the great lake, and Raven Wing not being very familiar with the country, having passed this way only once before, the trail had a zig zag pattern that led the party generally eastward.

Every evening the tired hunters would amble into camp carrying whatever they happened to harvest that day, and the next morning a different group would be sent out to scour the country, always moving in an eastwardly direction. Dividing the hunting chore kept the hunters from becoming exhausted. Roots and herbs supplemented their meals; a diet of meat alone became quickly monotonous.

The trackers made a wide detour around a Santee village located on the north shore of a small lake. Though the villagers were Falcon's distant relatives, the Norge wanted no confrontation, whether friendly or otherwise, to delay their journey.

As Raven Wing had predicted, they were one week to the day in completing the trip. They hadn't bothered trying to track Floki, knowing before hand what his destination would be. When the group came to an area that Raven Wing recognized as being only a league from his village, he suggested the Norge stay there while he went to talk to his father. The village was situated on the west bank of a small river that flowed from the north and emptied into the westernmost arm of the great lake.

Raven Wing planned to circle around and enter the village from the north, the farthest point from Floki's ship, which was anchored on the south side of the village. With the village in sight, he waited at the edge of the forest near the river until a group of boys with fishing spears came his way. When the boys came near enough to recognize him, Raven Wing spoke to them before revealing himself. Recognizing him, the youngsters came closer.

"Raven Wing! Everyone in the village believes you are dead. Your father will be happy to know that you are alive and well. Why are you here hiding behind that tree?" asked the nearest one of the group.

I have escaped from the evil palefaces. If they see me, they will surely kill me. I have no weapon with which to protect myself."

"Ha! Little do you know. They cannot see you, nor can they harm you. They are all dead! Our warriors killed them all, while losing not one man."

"Wah! Do not joke with me. How can such a thing be?"

"Go and talk with your father. He will want to see you."

"Yes, that is what I shall do. I want to know every detail of the battle. I want to hear how each one of them died."

Raven Wing had a difficult time trying to make his way to his father's lodge. Every person that saw him wanted an explanation as to where he had been and what had happened to him. In return he told each one to follow him and he would give his story so that all could hear at the same time.

Hearing the commotion created by the gathering crowd, Raven Wing's father, Chief Red Hawk, emerged from his lodge fully armed. When he recognized Raven Wing at the head of the procession, he dropped his weapons and rushed forward to greet his son. The chief's normally stoic attitude was completely abandoned in the excitement of the moment, as he clasped his son in a tight bear hug. Raven Wing was a little embarrassed at all the attention being lavished upon him.

"You are well my son?" asked Red Hawk, as he held Raven Wing at arm's length to better look upon his face.

"Yes, my father, I am in perfect health. Should I not be?"

"It was feared that you—uh--had maybe--met with harm, when it was discovered that you were not with the hairy ones."

"I refused to return with them, hoping that they would be killed when they came back without me. The chief of the palefaces that we had heard about gave me refuge in his village by the Red River. Tell me, my father, what happened when the evil ones arrived."

"You were correct in your belief that they would be killed, for that is exactly what happened."

"After you were taken hostage by the evil ones, I gave the order to clear every bush and small tree from all around the great canoe. I knew they would someday return, and I wanted to be ready for them."

"For the whole time that you were away, a warrior kept watch from aboard the great canoe each night, and another was posted near the beach. A few days ago, before dawn, the palefaces were discovered trying to sneak aboard the canoe. When the alarm was raised, all the warriors in the village, having been instructed to keep their bows handy, quickly responded to the call. The palefaces were surrounded in the open before they had a chance to flee. The sentry aboard the big canoe, being quite close to the enemy, was able to see by the moonlight that you were not among the palefaces. A volley of arrows was released into the closely packed group. It really wasn't much of a battle, and not a single one of our warriors was wounded."

"We found out later that one of the evil ones had been previously wounded. He remained in the tree line while the others stealthily tried for the great canoe. While the others were being brought down by the many arrows, that one clumsily tried to escape. He was taken alive. There is no need to tell you that he paid the penalty for the crimes of the whole group. There was much hatred for these men for what we thought they had done to you. Even though you are unharmed, would you not say that these men were even more evil than we first thought?"

"It makes my heart glad to hear this news. They were very evil men; they deserved to die. What did you do with the bodies, my father?"

"Since there was already much hatred for those men, and we took for granted that you had suffered at their hands, their bodies were turned over to the women who hacked them to pieces. The remains were thrown into the great canoe, covered with brush, and set afire. The burning craft, having been launched into the stream, was carried out into the bay, where it burned and sank."

"There were not as many of them as when you were forced to go with them. Do you know what happened to the other two?"

"One very bad man was turned over to the Sisseton tribe for crimes committed against two of their women. The other one, being a young man with a good heart, grew tired of following the evil ones and took refuge in the village of palefaces who live beside the Muddy River."

"It is all over at last. You are home safe and sound; we shall have a feast celebration in honor of your homecoming."

"There is one small matter that I must take care of first, Father. There is a group of my friends, palefaces from the western village, camped nearby. They are waiting for news concerning the evil ones. I must go to them and tell them what you have told me: that the evil ones are all dead."

"These men are friends of yours, and they are palefaces?"

"Yes, Father. They gave me refuge when I refused to return with the evil ones."

"For what purpose were these men seeking the ones who held you captive?"

"They would have killed them, Father. The evil ones took as many as two hands of their friends by surprise and slew them," explained Raven Wing, opening and closing his right hand twice. "That was when one of them was wounded."

"Your friends will also be my friends, my son. Go and invite them to come and celebrate with us. We will rejoice because you are safe; they can celebrate the justice that was brought to the ones they were seeking. Assure them, upon my word as chief and a grateful father, that they will be safe in this village."

"Thank you, my father. I shall leave immediately."

At first Steinn and the others were hesitant to accept the invitation, but an insistent Raven Wing prevailed over their objections, assuring the Norge over and over that his father would keep his word. Although Floki and all his men had met their deaths, many of the group were extremely disappointed that revenge had been snatched from their own hands. There was more than a little resentment felt toward the Cree, and Raven Wing could feel the coolness in their attitude, but he also understood why they would have such feelings.

In olden times Vikings were given an honorable funeral aboard a burning ship. The Cree, in their ignorance, had done for Floki what none of the Norge would have considered doing.

The celebration had already begun when the Norge cautiously entered the Cree village. They were greeted as welcomed guests with no sign of hostility. The tension of being among strangers soon dissipated and the men began to relax and enjoy the food and festive air of the occasion. The lack of communication was a problem, but it didn't prevent anyone from enjoying the festivities. The celebration continued on into the night until one by one the people became too tired to continue. To be on the cautious side, Steinn thought it best that his group stay close together throughout the night. They slept near the bonfire around which the celebration had taken place. Raven Wing took his rest with the group to reassure them that all would be right.

The next morning farewells were taken, and the Norge left the Cree village, headed west. Raven Wing walked along with the Norge a short distance in order to thank Steinn personally.

"I am grateful to you and your people for showing me so much kindness," he began, haltingly. "As long as my father and I are alive, you will be welcome in our village. Maybe someday I will come to visit you again. Goodbye my brother."

"You and your people will ever be welcomed as friends in the Norge village. Visit us any time you wish. May the Great Spirit watch over you, always."

Everyone was anxious to return to the village, having been away so long. The Cree village had supplied each man with enough dried meat and fish to last several days, cutting the return trip by two days. Steinn, too, was looking forward to a good meal cooked by a woman and an extended rest until he suddenly remembered, upon espying the palisade wall, that he was now a married man. The memory of a stranger in his lodge put a damper on his elation at being home again.

The women of the village began immediately to prepare a special meal in honor of the tired and hungry men. Rosebud was as actively engaged as the other women in the preparation of the food. She seems to have been fully accepted by the other women, and if she had any homesickness, it didn't show. Steinn found himself watching the girl as she carried on her duties; she was really quite attractive he realized.

Before the meal had finished cooking, most of the tired men, including Steinn, had fallen asleep. They had to be awakened when it was time to eat. Rosebud served Steinn personally, bringing him the choicest pieces of meat she could find. She smiled coyly at him as she placed a wooden bowl filled with bison stew into his hands. Steinn thanked her, and judging from her actions, she seemed to understand what he had said. He found out later that Helga, knowing from her own experience how important communication can be, had been working diligently to teach Rosebud as many Norge words as possible during his absence.

After the meal was over, Steinn wanted nothing more than to go to his bed and sleep until he was fully rested. He entered his lodge and lay down fully clothed and would have been asleep in short order, except that Rosebud, who had followed closely behind him, held her nose, and pointing at his moccasins and buckskins, insisted that he disrobe. No one in the party of men had had an opportunity to bathe in two weeks. Small wonder they stank. Steinn, feeling very self-conscious kept his back turned toward a seemingly non-caring Rosebud, as he shucked his stinking clothes.

Rosebud unceremoniously piled the clothes outside the lodge door and walked away. Steinn, thinking that he could now go to sleep, lay back down, but before sleep came, he was roused grumbling from his bed again. Rosebud had returned from Helga's lodge with a wooden bucket filled with hot water and a small piece of lye soap made from bison fat and hickory ashes, with a pleasant-smelling herbal fragrance added.

Since night had fallen, Steinn had only to step outside to bathe. After Rosebud wet him down, he soaped himself, and then let her rinse the soap from his body. She picked up the dirty clothes and as she was about to return the bucket, she pointed at the doorway of the lodge and said: "Sleep."

Rosebud washed the smelly moccasins with soap and water and placed them away from the fire. If they completely dried before Steinn wore them again, they would shrink and become stiff. He would have to form them to his feet while they were still damp. After building a simple rack over a small cedar fire, she draped Steinn's clothes so that the fragrant smoke would permeate them.

Taking another bucket of warm water, Rosebud bathed herself with the fragrant soap. Carrying the clothes and moccasins inside the lodge, a quarter of the night had passed before Rosebud could finally get into bed. She quietly crawled under the cover and snuggled close to her sleeping husband. She hoped he would be pleasantly surprised when he awoke in the morning.

As dawn was breaking the next morning, Steinn's mind was still in a sleepy fog as he shifted position. Feeling bare flesh next to him, he came instantly awake. Steinn was in the process of slipping from under the covers when Rosebud turned to him with a big smile and said in halting Norge: "Gut—marning—usban."

"Uh, good morning to you, too, Rosebud, uh, wife. Excuse me, I—there is something that I must do outside."

"Gum—bok," said Rosebud, patting the place where Steinn had slept.

"Yes—I'll be back in just a minute," said Steinn, as he wrapped a bison robe around his shoulders.

When Steinn returned, he slipped back under the covers and Rosebud came willingly into his arms.

IX

It was time to begin preparations for winter. A great herd of bison had gathered on the other side of the Red River and was beginning to wend its way slowly southward. Steinn, knowing that Knutson and his men had never been on a bison hunt, asked if they would like to participate in the harvesting of meat.

"Since we will be living in this land from now on, there will be other hunts that we can take part in," Knutson replied. "My men and I have talked it over, and we would like to go back to the lake and help by laying in a supply of fish for the winter. We—some of us—still have nightmares about what happened. The only way to cure such a malady is to face it head on. We are already experienced fishermen; we can become bison hunters later."

"If that is what you wish, I am agreeable. You will probably need some extra men to keep the drying fires going. I will ask for volunteers, but most of the men would rather go hunting, so I may have to assign some of them to go with you. I'll take Erik, the former Floki crewman, with me. There's no need to take a chance on his presence rubbing your men the wrong way. He had no part in the massacre, but his being among your crew might be like rubbing salt on a wound. So far, he has shown every sign of trying to make amends for his former life, but only time will tell just how serious he is."

"If there is nothing else, then, we will go our separate ways at daybreak. Good luck on the fishing."

Steinn would have to go as far west to reach the bison herd, as Knutson would have to go east to fish. He hoped there would be no trouble; they all needed a long rest after the hectic days just past. All the trouble of the past few weeks seems to have come at once, coinciding with the arrival of Floki. Steinn would never forgive himself for not taking a stronger stand against Floki, but he really had no idea just how depraved the man was. Steinn wanted nothing more than to live in peace, but he could now see that peace sometimes can be preserved only by showing a willingness to fight.

The responsibility of leading a whole village was burdensome, but now Steinn had a wife to consider as well. With every day that passed he grew closer to Rosebud. Now that he was certain that she was not with child as a result of the rape, he was greatly relieved. That knowledge had a great deal to do with his changed attitude toward her. In time Steinn knew that he could relegate the rape incident to the back of his mind, especially since he would not have to rear a child that belonged to Olaf the Pig, as he now thought of the man.

None of the Norge knew exactly how Olaf had died, since Falcon no longer visited the village of his birth, but then, none of them really cared. Life had returned to normal with the departure of Floki, and that was the way everyone wanted things to be.

The sighting of the bison herd wiped all worries from Steinn's mind. The hunters donned the wolf skins and began the slow stalking of their prey. The primal feeling that welled up in Steinn's breast made him want to howl like the wolf that had provided the disguise he now wore. Two-dozen animals had been easily brought down, but then the actions of the herd suddenly changed. In order to investigate the growing alarm demonstrated by some of the bison, Steinn backed off several steps before coming fully erect. He could see several hundred paces away, in the direction from which the bison were coming, a band if native men who were attempting to stampede the herd.

Steinn groaned inwardly, knowing that since the natives had never before shown such bravado, that trouble was imminent. Falcon, also sensing the change in the herd, came to where Steinn was standing. "Those men are from my father's village. I will go talk with them to see why they are doing this thing."

"I know these are your people, but it may not be safe to go alone. You're one of us now," said Steinn.

"I cannot say for sure if it is safe or not. Obviously, something has changed, since nothing like this has happened before. We will stay a safe distance away, just in case."

"Do you think this may be connected with Olaf? I was hoping that incident was completely settled."

"We shall find out, shortly," said Falcon, as he made his way toward the band of warriors.

Steinn told the other hunters, all of whom had come to see what was taking place, to take a few more bison if possible. The meat would be necessary for their survival through the winter, no matter what difficulties may arise today. The group of native warriors was not large enough to attack the Norge hunting party. The worst that they could do at the moment would be to interfere with the meat harvest.

Falcon and Steinn halted 50 paces from the warriors. "*Hau,* brothers," Falcon said in greeting.

"Hunn! You dare call us brothers, while standing beside a pale skin? Are you not also helping them kill the bison that *Wakan Tanka* has provided for his children?" said the apparent leader of the group.

"It is my belief that *Wakan Tanka* created all men, making all of us his children, and there are more than enough bison to meet all our needs."

"This land is the hunting ground of the seven allied tribes of which you used to belong."

"I have not forgotten my people. I am still Lakota."

"You hunt with the pale skins; you live with the pale skins; you have taken a wife from among the pale skins. What more need I say?"

"Forget about me. Tell me, why the sudden change toward the Norge? Why are you attempting to stampede the bison herd?"

"Since the news has reached our village that the Cree have killed 10 of the pale skins without losing a single warrior, the Seven Council Fires have met. Now, everyone knows that there is no magic in the weapons of the Norge, as we had once feared. The decision was made to take back our hunting and fishing grounds. As you know, winter is a bad time to make war. You live with the Norge, Falcon, but I am telling you now, leave their village before spring begins, or you will die with them."

The spokesman of the group, having made his point, turned and walked away; the others followed. Falcon and Steinn made their way back to the other hunters, where Falcon related what had taken place. Steinn, who had heard everything but had no idea what had been said, sadly shook his head. The peace that he had so diligently sought with the natives had just taken a giant leap away from him.

Since there seemed to be no immediate threat, Steinn went to where Rosebud was working over a fat bison cow and began to help her with the butchering. Hours later, with all the meat sliced from the bones and loaded on travois, the long trek back to the village was begun. Steinn was downcast on the homeward journey, but only Rosebud seemed to notice. With everyone being in such a festive mood, Steinn decided to let them enjoy themselves until after they had feasted on the fresh meat before revealing the decision that he had come to.

The first person Steinn saw when he crossed the river was Knutson. After all the evil of the past weeks, Steinn braced himself for more bad news; Knutson, he regretted, did not disappoint him.

Steinn…we went to the lake and found the boats, they were exactly where we abandoned them the day that we fled from Floki, but somebody had been there before us. The boats were completely demolished. Not one single board was salvageable. There was nothing to do but return empty handed.

Steinn related to Knutson what had occurred during the bison hunt.

"I am not surprised about the boats. After everyone has eaten, we need to discuss the future. Nothing will ever again be the same around here."

Steinn tried to put on an air of cheerfulness, but his mind kept returning to the events of the day. He knew they would have to leave this area, and soon. The natives had never been exactly friendly, but neither had they been overtly hostile. Well, he had tried his best to keep the peace, and his success had been high, but he had failed to figure Floki into the equation. Who could have foreseen that the man would destroy in a matter of days everything the Norge had worked years to establish? And to think that out of all the things he had done, the final act of being killed was the worst. By dieing, while the natives suffered no loss, he had given them the courage to become belligerent.

As the feast showed signs of breaking up, Steinn stood up and asked for everyone's attention. After explaining to the people that didn't know about the confrontation with the warriors at the bison hunt and Knutson's findings at the lake, he asked if there was anyone that did not grasp the seriousness of their predicament. All the people seemed subdued by the information; no one took the situation lightly.

"Does anybody have anything to add to what I have said? No? Does anyone not agree that we cannot stay here? No? Then we need to make plans to leave before spring. If we leave here early enough and everything goes well, we can arrive at our destination in time to put in a maize crop. Now, first of all, we have to have a supply of fish and rice to augment the bison harvest. I suggest we take four boats to Bison Lake at the head of the river. Since we haven't fished there in a couple of years, the fish have had a chance to replenish themselves. Four boats should carry enough men to deter an attack by the natives, but if we have to fight, we will. Is this agreeable to everyone? Then I'll leave the selection of the men to Knutson, Rolf, Pall, and Falcon. Include me in one of the boats. We leave first thing in the morning.

Rosebud snuggled close to her husband that night. She was so proud of her man. Not only was he impressive in size, he was forceful when he had to be, and so brave. She had feared for him when he had confronted the warriors from her village, her very own kinfolk. She had not been concerned for the warriors at all. Did that mean that she was now Norge instead of Sisseton? Yes, she believed that was true. She enjoyed a life here in the Norge village that she had not had in her childhood home. No longer did she even think of her former life; it seemed but a dim memory, now. She was learning the Norge language, so communication was becoming less of a problem, she had friends, and she had a husband. Yes, she told herself with a newfound sense of pride, she was now Norge.

The leaders of the fishing expedition decided that two extra boats would be needed to haul the catch back to the village. There would be a total of forty men altogether. Twelve men were taken from the first four boats and divided into two crews to row the two extra boats to the lake.

The fishing party, after camping a night beside the Bison River, rowed into the small lake at the head of the river and immediately let out their nets. After the first haul of fish, the crews of two of the boats began to gather wood and prepare drying racks. Those guarding the camp swapped positions on a regular basis with the ones chopping wood and preparing fish, so that no one would have a reason to gripe.

After five days the men on the lake stopped netting fish and spent the next two days gathering rice, while the men on shore finished curing the catch. So far, no natives had been sighted, but the sentries remained alert, and when the drying was completed and the boats loaded, everyone was glad to be on the way home. The trip back was faster and easier, but darkness had fallen before they finally reached the village.

With maize, rice, dried squash, meat, and fish the Norge were well stocked for winter. There would still be the occasional deer taken before the worst winter weather began, but there was nothing much left to do except gather a supply of firewood.

Falcon had planned to start his next copper axe immediately after the negotiations with Rosebud's father, but events had piled up, one on top of the other, preventing any kind of leisure activity. To falcon, the making of an axe was tedious but enjoyable labor. Red Axe, rightly believing his prize to be unique, would not approve of another ornate axe being made. More than likely, he would never know about the second axe.

Steinn, having a useless brass spindle whorl, since there was no wool to spin, and a small cache of bronze coins inherited from his father that were worthless in this land, gave the items to Falcon to add to the copper. The color of the new axe would be different from the first one, and it would also be a little harder than the pure copper of the original. Steinn intended to help Falcon in any way he could, after all, he was responsible for the loss of the first axe.

Falcon wanted to do most of the task by himself, but he did allow Steinn to prepare the charcoal for the forge and the mold for the axe. The first example had been of a simple wedge shape; the new axe had more flare at the cutting edge, and the color was a lustrous orange. The handle Falcon carved into the form of a cormorant neck and head. The finished product, in his opinion, was even more beautiful than the first. Everyone in the village came to admire Falcon's handiwork; all admitting the axe was exquisite.

The women kept busy throughout the winter working with the animal hides, fashioning new moccasins, leggings, shirts, dresses, and robes. The men hunted, made new weapons or repaired old ones, and fitted the boats with outriggers for the journey to the Smoking River.

Steinn and Falcon in their discussions had many times gone over the route that must be taken to the west. If the people could walk all the way, leaving the boats and most of their possessions behind, the journey would be directly west and much shorter, but Steinn nor anyone else would even consider such a thing. The route planned would be far longer and require more time to negotiate, but the trek should be possible in six weeks at the most.

Falcon had never been as far west as the Smoking River, but he had been close. Once, when he was 12 summers old, his father and several other men and their sons had visited the Teton, a kindred tribe that had migrated onto the prairie. There was nothing remarkable about the journey that he could recall, until one reached the low plateau not far from the Smoking River that was a more broken land than the undulating slopes of the prairie. He knew from conversations with the men of his tribe that the Sheyenne River had its very beginnings in the hills of the plateau. How difficult the passage would be through these hills he did not know; only time would tell.

Nothing can stop the passage of time, and as the day of departure drew closer, the people became more restive. Tempers flared and arguments abounded, making Steinn's life as arbitrator in most of the cases, a misery. Everybody knew what was causing the problem, but they seemed powerless to do anything about it. This place had been home to them for several years, and no one wanted to leave, but what other choice did they have? Even though they were argumentive, they loved one another and would like to continue the life they now lived. Yet, from the very beginning of their sojourn at this site, they were reluctant to build large earth houses, knowing they might have to leave at any time. That knowledge hidden in the recesses of their minds didn't make the actual leaving any easier.

Early in April, Steinn figured the time had come to leave. Everything of real value was loaded into the boats. Many items had to be left behind; there was no room for anything but the necessities of life. Some of the people kept dragging their feet, delaying the departure as long as possible, until Steinn came close to losing his patience.

Finally, all the adults and older children had been ferried to the western shore of the Muddy River, and the old and the very young took their places in the boats. There not being enough room in the boats for everyone, most of the people would have to walk. Six men were chosen as rowers for each boat. The first leg of the journey would be the longest, but from that time on, each morning others would be chosen to take their places. Like every other able-bodied man in the party, Steinn would take his turn at rowing. He didn't want anyone to have an excuse to gripe. There had been enough of that already.

The Sheyenne River made a huge bend to the south before turning to the west, and then north for many leagues before turning again to the west. Those on foot must walk 25 leagues directly west to arrive at the same spot on the river that those in the boats would have to travel 60 leagues to reach. No fighting men were sent to escort the boats--there being enough well armed rowers to deter any native attack. Steinn assigned one man the task of keeping the boats tightly grouped. This man would bring up the rear to make sure there were no stragglers.

The spring rains had not come yet but rowing upstream at any time is always hard work. When the two groups came back together, a whole day and night of rest was granted to the tired rowers. From this point until they came to the Smoking River, the group would remain together. According to Falcon the Sheyenne village, if it was still there, was probably five days away, but sentries would be posted every night from now until the Norge reached their destination.

After four more days of travel, Falcon scouted ahead to locate the Sheyenne village. It was still there, he reported, on the north side of the river--the same side that the main body of the Norge were on. It would not be wise for a large group of armed men to walk through the center of the village, even though it appeared from the number of lodges that the Sheyenne would be outnumbered.

"We can ask for permission to pass through, or we can cross the river and pass on the other side. Either way, I suggest we make contact with them. If they are taken by surprise, they may attack. What do you think, Steinn?"

"Yes, I agree with you. Since you know sign language, Falcon, you are the only one able to communicate with them. Take a group of men of your choosing with you, but keep them in the background, so that they won't appear as a threat. Tell their leader that we are passing through, and that we will cross to the other side of the river to allay any fear of attack that they may have.

Every native in the village turned out to watch the boats carrying the pale skinned strangers go by. They had heard of the strange red and yellow haired people who lived on the Red River, but no one from the village had dared venture close enough to the compound to get a good look at them. The children in the boats waved at the children on the riverbank, and they in turn shyly waved back.

If given the chance, those children would play together without prejudice or animosity. It was only after people grew older that they learned from others to hate their fellow man, whether because of skin color, nationality, religion, or any other difference. As Steinn stood on the opposite bank from the natives, he thought that these two races, looking so different from each other, wanted exactly the same thing out of life: a chance to pursue happiness.

That night a heavier guard than usual was posted, but morning dawned without incident. The Norge party marched steadily westward, with a squad of heavily armed men on each side of the river acting as a rear guard. Although the Sheyenne had shown no hostility as the Norge had passed the village, Steinn was taking no chances. At the midday break, a runner from the squad across the river rushed into camp, pointing and exclaiming excitedly about a dust cloud approaching from the east. Only a large group of people or animals on the move could stir up so much dust.

Steinn posted lookouts all around the perimeter of the camp, but the main body of fighting men hurriedly crossed the river, where they were deployed to meet the threat approaching from the rear. In case a battle ensued, he kept 20 men in reserve, hidden in a willow thicket along the river, to be used wherever the need may arise.

Falcon, well hidden in the growth along the river, was several hundred yards in front from the Norge line. He waited until the makers of the dust cloud were clearly discernable before revealing himself. From all appearances, the whole native village was on the move, and the chief of the Sheyenne was recognizable as the leader. As Falcon walked out of hiding with his right hand raised in the sign of peace, the natives came to a halt. The village chief, also with raised hand, walked to where Falcon was waiting. After a few minutes of signing, Falcon turned and walked toward where Steinn was waiting, and the village leader returned to his people.

"Steinn, these people are from the village we passed yesterday. Their chief is called Broken Hand; you can't help knowing the reason why when you meet him. It has been their desire for some time to go beyond the Smoking River to join their relatives on the other side; but being few in number, they were reluctant to make the move for fear of being caught at a disadvantage on the open prairie. The Seven Tribes have been putting pressure on them just as they were doing to us. For mutual protection, they would like to travel along with us, if you will permit it."

"Well, there's no doubt that we have them outnumbered. It would be foolish for them to start trouble, and since they are traveling with their women and children, I believe they are sincere. Sure, why not? The greater the number of fighting men, the safer we will all be. Go tell them they are welcome to join us at our camp.

"Broken Hand says it might be better if his people remain on this side of the river until we all get to know one another better. When the river plays out in a few more days, they will join us."

"Well, whatever he thinks best. Let's go talk to him; I should get to know the man, since he is going to be traveling with us."

Falcon was right about the chief's hand thought Steinn, but he had failed to mention the rest of the chief's body. The left hand of the old man that was limping toward him looked more like a claw than a human hand. Steinn tried to ignore the maimed hand, but it was hard not to glance at it occasionally. The movement of the hand being limited made signing more difficult, but the chief was able to make himself understood. Steinn could detect no animosity in the old man, convincing him that the chief was sincere and only had the best interest of his people at heart.

The chief was a short man, being no more than five and a half feet tall, but he was heavily built. The shape of the hand and the way he carried it was noticeable at a distance, but the hand was only one of the chief's impairments. He had only one eye, the left one, and his nose had evidently been crushed, as it was wide and flat. There were multiple scars on the old man's face, and Steinn wondered what the rest of his body must look like. The limping gait of the old man obviously meant another injury. From all the evidence, Steinn figured the chief must have been caught in a bison stampede.

The men, women, and children kept inching closer to get a closer look at the red-haired giant that towered above their chief. None of them had ever before seen a man over six feet tall, and this hairy stranger was six inches beyond that. Most of Broken Hand's followers were a little fearful of the pale strangers, but their chief was a wise leader and would not expose them to unnecessary danger.

The noon break had lasted much longer than was first intended. There was only two more hours left before sundown, so Steinn raised his voice loud enough to be heard across the river, saying that they would camp where they were for the night and to unload one of the boats to ferry the men back across the river. They didn't want to get wet again this close to nightfall.

After two more days of rowing, the Sheyenne River began to dwindle in size. Shoals became more frequent as the land began to steadily rise toward the highlands, making the flow swifter and harder to row against. The decision was made to take the boats from the water and skid them across the prairie from here to the Smoking River.

Broken Hand brought his people across a shoal to join the Norge on the south side of the river. Steinn, with Falcon's help, questioned the chief about the lay of the land and the best route through the hills to the west. The Sheyenne were very familiar with this area, it being part of their hunting grounds, so Steinn asked the chief if he would take the lead through the broken land ahead.

Four rawhide ropes, two short ones and two longer ones, were attached to each boat. With four men pulling, and the women and children pushing, the boats moved across the prairie with amazing ease.

The Sheyenne women, children, and dogs pulled travois of various sizes loaded with the tribe's earthly possessions. The warriors of the clan, always on the alert, carried only their weapons. Some of the Norge men, being tethered to the boats like dray horses, were envious of the warriors, but no one openly griped, since they knew how Steinn felt about complainers. Besides, every Norge man, including Steinn, took a turn at the towing, giving no one an excuse to complain.

The procession had been under way for less than an hour before Steinn had to intercede in a dispute. At the first down grade, one of the boats—pushed by boys full of energy and not yet tiring of the work, which in the early stages was like a game to them—overtook one of the men ahead, knocking him down and pinning his right ankle under an outrigger. One of the boys laughed when the man went down but stopped when he realized the seriousness of what had happened. The man, in pain and rage, was cursing the boy that had laughed, while feeling all around for something, anything to throw at him. Luckily for the youngster, who was slowly backing away from the ranting man, the ground was stone free.

Two of the other men lifted the side of the boat enough to free the man's ankle. There was some bruising and loss of skin, but no bones were broken. The man would probably be exempt from towing for a day or two, and he would limp for a while, but he would soon heal.

Steinn had to come between the injured man, still angry and wanting revenge, and the father of the boy who didn't like the cursing being directed at his son. It took a while, but Steinn finally quieted the angry man, and looking out over the crowd that had gathered, promised them that if such an incident happened again that he would personally take a switch to the guilty party. All of them, young and old, took him seriously, and there were no more incidents.

As the trekkers penetrated deeper into the hills and buttes, the Sheyenne River began to branch off left and right, and with each branch the main stream became smaller. A well-worn bison trail crossed and re-crossed the diminishing stream until over half of the way through the hills had been negotiated, then the trail led up and over a divide into the watershed of a small westward flowing stream. Since the way was now downhill, pushing the boats was no longer required. Three days after taking the boats out of the Sheyenne River, the journey to the great Smoking River was completed.

None of the Norge had ever seen such a great river before. The river they had entered upon leaving the northern sea had been big, but nothing like this one before them now. The river was low at this time of the year, and there was only intermittent fog, making the far shore quite discernable: a condition he had been told that would change with the coming of the hot humid days of summer.

Between the river and the hills, a level place of only a few acres in size was found. Here, the group set up a temporary camp, intending to stay only long enough to rest. The Norge built temporary lean-to type shelters, while the Sheyenne erected the skin and pole lodges they had brought with them from the plains. Hunters of both clans were sent north and south along the river to harvest whatever animals were available in the area, while the women gathered edible roots and plants.

The men brought in enough deer and elk to have a great feast. Two large pots of a savory stew were cooked, along with roasted meat, stewed roots and vegetables, and a basket of dried berries that had clung to the bushes throughout the winter for dessert. Everyone was in a festive mood; almost as if reaching the river was the goal they had been striving for. No talk of future plans was forthcoming; they simply wanted to enjoy the day. Tomorrow would be soon enough for decision making.

The two clans couldn't communicate well enough to converse with each other, but that didn't keep them from mingling. Falcon and Rosebud, who knew enough sign language to get by, were kept busy interpreting for various groups attempting to haggle over some trade item. The Sheyenne were interested in any item made of steel, while the Norge sought items of clothing made from animal skins. Every Sheyenne woman would love to have one of the large iron or copper pots, but the Norge wouldn't even consider parting with such a valuable item. When the ones they now owned were used up or broken, there would be no more.

Guards were posted, even though everyone felt secure here with the hills to their back and the river to the front. The night passed without incident, and after a breakfast of leftovers, Steinn suggested that they empty the boats and ferry the Sheyenne across the river. The natives were readily agreeable to this plan. The lodge poles posed the greatest problem to conveyance. They would interfere with the rowers if hauled lengthwise in the boats; the ends dipping in the water hindered the guiding of the boats when loaded crosswise; and if lashed together and towed behind a boat, the current kept the boat pointed upstream, making rowing diffi-cult. Finally, it was decided to make one large bundle of poles, and to keep it from rolling in the water, an outrigger was lashed to the downstream side of the bundle. With four Sheyenne men astride the bundle with paddles, the craft could be rowed like a canoe, which they were familiar with.

By midday all the natives and their possessions were on the western shore of the river. As the last boat was unloaded, there were tears of sadness coursing down the cheeks of some of the native women because of friendships made during the short time with the Norge, and because two of the young unmarried Shey-enne women, having found mates among the unattached men of Knutson's group, would be left behind.

Steinn had made a point of being in the last boat to unload. He wanted to say goodbye to Broken Hand and his people, hop-ing for a lasting friendship with the tribe. After Steinn, Falcon, and Broken Hand had said their farewells, the elderly chief faced Steinn and began to sign.

"Do not delay your departing from this place," Falcon trans-lated. "The days are becoming warmer and the snow in the Shining Mountains far to the west are even now beginning to melt. The melt water combined with spring rains will turn this river into a mighty, raging torrent I am sure that you have never seen anything like it. Great trees, uprooted when the riverbanks collapse, will come sweeping by. I have seen small herds of bison drowned, when for whatever reason, they tried to cross the flooded river. It is truly a frightening thing to behold. Try to be at your destination before this begins."

"Thank you, Broken Hand,; you are a true friend. May the Creator of all men always smile upon you. But before we depart, let me ask you a question. Have you ever heard tell of a people of my race somewhere to the south along this river?"

"Yes. Rumors of a different race of men driven from the lands to the east have reached my ears, but I do not know if they are true, you understand."

"Do you know how far away these people would be?"

"No. Only that it is very far away. That is all that I know."

"Thank you once again, my friend."

Steinn called a meeting immediately after returning to camp, the information that Broken Hand had imparted about the river causing him deep concern. He decided to keep the information to himself for the time being; there was no need to frighten the people unnecessarily.

"There is no way that all of us can travel in the few boats we have, and there is not enough time to fabricate more. To travel by land on this side of the river is out of the question. The other side looks to be more open and level, but time is of the utmost importance. We need to arrive at our destination, get settled, and plant our crops. All of this will take many days to accomplish, too much time to travel by land."

Our destination lies far downstream from here. According to Broken Hand there is a white race of people rumored to have migrated from the east and settled on the Smoking River. If we can find these people, maybe our search for a permanent home will end.

"Now, looking back to our departure from Greenland as an example, I suggest we make a raft large enough to carry all the people and their possessions. With everyone working together, the project shouldn't take very long. We will need a lot of strong rope to lash the logs together. The women can start immediately cutting our excess hides into strips. The men can begin to fell trees, and the bigger boys can cut poles to serve as cross members and dowel pins. I envision a raft long and narrow, which should make it more manageable in the current. Also, with several boats tethered by ropes of various lengths to the upstream end of the raft, we should be able, by rowing backward, to guide the raft, control the rate of our descent on the river, and possibly even be able to stop in midstream if necessary. Does anyone have anything to add? No? Then let's get started."

Steinn oversaw the building of the raft; Knutson took control of the tree cutting; and Rolf coordinated the snaking of the logs to the river. Steinn was amazed at how well the people were working together and how fast the raft was taking shape. By nightfall the project, Steinn estimated, was probably one-third completed.

Sometime during the night Steinn was awakened by raindrops that had penetrated the lean-to roof and were dripping on his face. The hastily erected shelter was really more of a windbreak than a dwelling. He pulled the cover over his head and went back to sleep. The rain fell without ceasing all the next day, slowing the construction of the raft, and causing Steinn much consternation. If the rain was falling in the mountains to the west, the snow would melt that much faster. Well, worrying wouldn't help. If the river became un-navigable, they would just have to establish themselves in a good location and delay their journey for another year. His people should be no worse off living beside this river than they were at the compound on the Red River.

By late afternoon, the rain came to an end. Steinn had, after arising that morning, driven a stick into the ground at the water's edge. It was hard to say, because of the lapping of small waves that were created by the wind, whether the river was higher or not. If it had risen, it wasn't much, but then, there had been no downpour, just a steady drizzle. And too, it would take time for snowmelt to come all this way from the mountains. He didn't know how far away the mountains were, but they couldn't be seen from his present position.

Throughout the years beside the Red River, Steinn had taken the rise and fall of the water with the seasons for granted, but the Red being a small river was navigable even at flood stage. If Broken Hand hadn't gone into detail about this great river in flood, Steinn, because of ignorance, would not now be worried. But the knowledge of what could happen made him anxious to have this journey over with, and soon. The thought of the raft with so many people aboard being swamped in a raging flood made him shudder. The old and the young would be utterly helpless in such a catastrophe. He tried unsuccessfully to concentrate on building the raft to keep such visions out of his mind.

By midmorning of the following day, the raft was finished and loading had begun. A final check of the camping area was made to see if any tools were lying about. The crews for the boats were chosen and the order to cast off was given. Steinn took a position at the rear of the raft to coordinate the rowing of the boats until the men at the oars got the feel of the job they were to do. The oarsmen pulling on the left-hand oars only, sent the raft slowly toward midstream. Once a safe distance from the shore, the rowers had only to keep the tethers to the raft taut and let the river do the work. The raft, being tied together by ropes was flexible, making it feel like a living thing beneath their feet. Two men with long poles at the front of the raft maintained a sharp lookout for snags and sandbars.

Soon everyone was working together without having to be guided and the tenseness that had gripped passengers and crew alike began to dissipate. Everything was going smoothly, and Steinn breathed a great sigh of relief.

Each morning two boats were sent ahead to scout the river for danger and to choose the best place to stop for the night. If a particularly hazardous area were encountered, one boat and crew would stay to guide the raft through, while the other would continue down the river. Each evening a relatively calm area of the river, usually on the downstream side of a sandbar, was chosen to moor the raft. Most of the smaller boats were kept tied to the raft.

As several small villages had been seen on both sides of the river, the raft was never moored within arrow range of the high, cliff-like banks. Sentries were posted each night, but no attack was ever made, and the party continued downstream unmolested.

In the middle of the afternoon of the ninth day, both scout boats were waiting at a good mooring site for the raft to arrive. A large village had been sighted on the south bank of a substantial clear running stream that entered the Smoking River from the west. Having seen smoke far ahead on the horizon, the boat crews went ashore and observed the village from the top of a hill. The crew-men were convinced that no one in the village had seen them, but from such a distance, they couldn't see the villagers with any detail either. They could see that the dwellings in the village were unlike any that they had encountered on the plains. From a distance, the lodges appeared to be identical to the earth houses made by the Norge for hundreds of years, only smaller. From this evidence alone the scouts were convinced that this must be the people they were seeking. Tomorrow, contact would be attempted. If all went well, their journey would be over.

The remainder of the afternoon Steinn spent going over in his mind how best to approach the village downstream and what to say once he got there. He was assuming of course that this was the right place and people. From the time that he had first heard about another pale skinned race in this new land, he had taken for granted that the Norge would be allowed to join them. Now that the meeting of these people was near, doubts were creeping into his mind. How could he be sure that he wouldn't be killed on sight? What would happen to his people if he were killed? Why had these thoughts never entered his mind before?

Europeans, although of the same race and religion, had been fighting and killing each other since time immemorial. The fact that these people, even more so than the Norge, had suffered per-secution by the native population and had been violently driven from their homeland did not mean that they would be sympathetic toward the Norge. There had never been any reason for him to think that his people would be welcomed with open arms. These strangers may feel no racial kinship at all for others of light skin. Well, it was too late to turn back now. Tomorrow would supply the answers to all his questions.

Steinn hardly slept at all that night, and when morning came, he was still tired--in mind and body. Throughout the night he had tossed and turned with every horrible scene that could be imagined entering his mind. His concern was not so much for himself but for his people. He wished now that he had followed the Sheyenne tribe to their homeland. At least they were friendly, and because of them, maybe the rest of their nation would have accepted the Norge.

He decided to take only Falcon with him to the village. If trouble arose, the fewer he had with him the better. Because he knew sign language, Falcon would have to be present to communicate with the strangers, otherwise, Steinn would rather go alone.

When the time to leave drew near, Steinn got everyone's attention. "People, if this mission fails, you must leave this area with all haste. You cannot go back upstream, and to leave here on foot would probably be disastrous. From what we know that is a large village with probably many warriors who would soon overtake you. The only choice left would be to continue down the river for a safe distance before establishing yourselves as well as possible."

"We know that the only friends we have for sure are Broken Hands people, but they are far to the north. If necessary, maybe contact with them would be possible. I am going to leave Paul Knutson and Rolf in charge just in case I don't return, but hopefully everything will turn out well."

"Now, I believe that we should join hands and ask God to bless this mission. We need His help and guidance, for on this day as never before, our future hangs in the balance. Paul, if you would do us the honor, please lead us in prayer."

With the ending of the prayer, Steinn said goodbye to a tearful Rosebud while trying to instill in her a confidence that he did not himself feel. Steinn entered the boat first, and because Falcon had little experience with oars, Steinn took the rowing position. One of the bystanders gave the boat a push, and they were on their way.

Steinn turned the boat so that he could face downstream, pulling on a right or left oar as needed to keep the boat straight with the current, and let the flow carry the boat stern first toward their goal. After an hour of riding the current, the smoke from many fires could be seen rising beyond a curve in the river. In a few more minutes the largest village that Steinn had ever seen came into view. If he was anywhere close in his judgment, there must be 2,000 people in this town. He silently prayed that these people were friendly; otherwise, the Norge would never stand a chance.

The town occupied the triangle of land between the Smoking River and a clear stream of substantial size flowing from the west. Steinn guided the boat into the mouth of the smaller river toward a series of wide steps carved into the riverbank. Apparently, this is where the people came to fetch water; as there were no boats of any kind moored there, it couldn't be a boat landing.

Steinn turned the boat so that Falcon could step ashore holding the tether rope from the prow. Tying the rope to an exposed root on the upstream side of the steps, the two very nervous men ascended the steps to where a large group of men, women, and children awaited them. The men were unarmed, which to Steinn was a good omen.

At the top of the steps were several peculiar skin-covered objects that looked very much like huge inverted cooking pots.

They would learn later that these were bullboats, the watercraft of this village.

Steinn saw immediately that these people were not like the members of other tribes he had encountered. Many of the men had beards, as well as light skin and brown hair. There were also people with the straight black hair and dark eyes that he had come to associate with the natives of this land. If these were former members of the Missouri tribe, an offshoot of the Winnebago and distant kin of Falcon, maybe he would be able to communicate with them verbally.

"Hau," said Falcon, holding his palm up and forward in the sign of greeting.

"Hau," came the reply from many of the people.

"I am called Falcon of the Sisseton sept of the Lakota nation, offspring of the Winnebago. This man is called Steinn. He is chief of the Norge people. We have come from far away to the northeast." In case his words were unintelligible to these people, Falcon used sign language while he spoke. "Do any of you understand my language?"

After looking at one another to see who the spokesman would be, one of the men with native features stepped forward, his lithe, muscular body and long, straight hair glistening with oil. "Many of your words are familiar, but it would be better if you continued to sign as well. My name is Raging Bull, chief of the Missouri faction of this village. This man is Snow Peak, chief of Lone Man's people. Together we are the *Numakiki,* the People. The tribes around us call us Mandan because of the red paint that we are so fond of. What is it that you seek in this village? We saw no trade goods in your strange canoe."

"No, we have not come here to trade. We are searching for a new place to make our homes. The powerful tribes of the northeast have driven us from our homeland. While we yet lived there, rumors came to our ears that another people had been driven from the valley of the Beautiful River to the east. We came from afar looking for that people. The Norge are few in number and want nothing more than a safe place to live and provide for our families."

"I see only two men. Where are your families?" Raging Bull asked warily.

"They are on the river north of this village."

Raging Bull spoke to the other members of the crowd, mostly the pale skin ones, who hadn't understood all the dialog with Falcon. There seemed to be growing alarm among the group, which was steadily increasing in number as news of the strangers spread throughout the village. What if these two had been sent to gather information about the village? Should these two be taken prisoners? Should preparations be made for an attack?

Falcon took this lull in the conversation to bring Steinn up to date on the proceedings.

"How numerous are your people?" Raging Bull asked, as Snow Peak, whose stocky body was topped by a mane of silver-gray hair, came to stand beside him.

"We number fewer than 500 people, including women and children."

"And the number of your warriors?"

"No more than 175 adult men."

Raging Bull visibly relaxed at this revelation. "Why should the *Numakiki* let your people live here?"

"There is safety in numbers. Have your people not suffered at the hands of a more powerful nation, even as we? If we are allowed to join you, your friends will be our friends; your enemies will be our enemies. Together, our numbers should be sufficient to discourage aggression by any other tribe."

Once again Raging Bull translated the proceedings to the others, while Falcon did the same for Steinn.

"My people, the Missouri, have known war with other tribes, but none have been strong enough to drive us from this land. The pale ones that you see here were driven from their homes far to the east. We have been as one people since they came here to live."

"Some of the People are curious about this man with you. They have never seen hair the color of autumn leaves before. It is obvious that you and he are very different. Where does such a one as he come from?"

"You and I are distant cousins, as both of our tribes are descended from the Winnebago, the grandfather of many tribes, but the Norge came in giant canoes from across the Sunrise Sea to this land, a journey of great distance I am told."

"Lone Man's people have an ancient tradition that they also came from across the Sunrise Sea in great winged canoes. I believed such tales mere myths until now. Maybe it is true after all."

"Allow me to speak to Snow Peak again. Since you are my distant cousin, maybe the bearded, pale skinned ones are his distant cousins."

The next few minutes seemed to drag by as Falcon and Steinn tried to fill the time by discussing the situation. These people, both agreed, seemed friendly enough. So far, no hostility had been detected by either of them. Both men earnestly hoped the search for a new home would end here.

"Snow Peak desires to know if Red Hair believes in Lone Man as the Creator of all men. If so, the Norge will be welcomed as cousins to become one with the People."

"Falcon, I have never heard of Lone Man, but do not tell that to Snow Peak. Tell him that my people believe that the One God created man; therefore, all men are children of the same father. The two names probably refer to the same Being, wouldn't you agree?"

"Yes. Obviously Lone Man as the Creator of all mankind would have to be more than a mere man. In my mind Lone Man, the One God, as well as the Great Spirit would all be one and the same. That is what I will tell him."

After speaking to Raging Bull and Snow Peak, Falcon turned to Steinn. "Snow Peak is satisfied with your answer. The reason that these two different people are able to live together in harmony is because Lone Man and the Great Spirit are viewed as one, making them brothers."

"He says that since most of the trees have been cut on the south side of the clear stream, building material and firewood is hard to come by. It might be better, he suggests, to build our lodges on the north shore. If either village came under attack, it would be no problem to send warriors across the river to help. He wants to know your opinion of this suggestion."

Steinn thought for only a moment. "Tell him that I approve the plan. We will be near enough for mutual protection, and our peoples will have a chance to get to know each other without being thrust together too suddenly. If the chiefs are agreeable, you and I will go bring the raft down."

What Steinn didn't say was that he would feel much safer with the river between the two villages, at least until the Mandan and Norge became familiar with each other. The Norge would be greatly outnumbered but could inflict many casualties if trouble flared up between the two tribes. The same thing might have been on the minds of Snow Peak and Raging Bull, bringing forth the suggestion of separate villages. If the Mandan and Norge were compatible, in time, through friendships and intermarriage, the two villages undoubtedly would become as one.

Steinn and Falcon clasped hands with the chiefs, and then descended the steps. The boat being too large for one man to row upstream, Steinn thought it better to cross to the north side of the clear river and walk back to the raft, a trek of only two leagues.

After leaving the boat, Steinn and Falcon walked over the site where their new village would be built. The land sloped gently away from the river for several hundred yards before rising more sharply. There was plenty of near--level farmland, and trees grew beside both rivers. The site Steinn decided was as good as any that could be found.

The people on the raft were relieved, as well as surprised, to see Steinn and Falcon appear on the high riverbank, as their return was expected from downstream in the boat. Some of the Norge having a negative outlook had believed the two men would never be seen alive again.

When Steinn announced that the journey was finally over, some of the people cried, some laughed and danced, while others knelt and prayed. Steinn waited until the celebrating was over, and then gave orders to untie the raft. In little more than an hour the huge craft was being maneuvered into the mouth of the clear stream. Curious Mandan lined the south bank, never having seen such a large raft before. A few of the bigger boys had crossed the river in the peculiar pot-like boats and were waiting for the Norge to arrive. Ropes at the front and rear of the raft were thrown to the waiting boys who tied them to exposed roots, securing the raft to the north bank.

The more impatient of the Norge clambered up the bank, using any hold available. At the top they turned and urged others to climb. "Wait!" Steinn yelled. "We will really have to struggle to unload the raft up such a steep bank. The first thing we need to do is to carve some steps, like the Mandan have done across the river. We will need access to the river for drinking water, as well as to our boats. I believe three men working abreast should make the steps wide enough. We'll take turns at the digging. Start at the top and work your way down."

With everyone anxious to get the raft unloaded and go ashore, the work went especially fast. Inside an hour a series of steps six feet wide descended the bank to the water's edge. Later the steps could be paved with flat stones to prevent slipping.

After taking his turn at digging, Steinn had kept busy planning the new village. Stakes were driven into the ground at each lodge site. The main street would be fifteen feet wide and begin at the top of the steps and run inland through the center of the village. One cross street of equal width would bisect the site in the other direction. The open space where the two streets intersected would be used as the town meeting place.

When everyone was assembled, each head of household, after consulting his spouse, was asked to choose the site for his new lodge. If two families chose to build a single lodge, Steinn didn't care. Single men could build their own dwelling or join with others; it didn't matter. The only thing that concerned Steinn was the arrangement of the lodges. They must be in orderly rows, not in a haphazard jumble.

Temporary shelters were quickly thrown up to keep their possessions dry. After the soil was broken up and the crops were in the ground, permanent houses would be built. Some of the Mandan having completed their own planting crossed the river to work beside the Norge, bringing pumpkin seeds and beans to share with their new neighbors. Steinn was amazed at how well things were going. It looked as if the Norge had finally found a home.

Already, members of the two villages, even though they couldn't communicate very well with each other, were freely crossing the river to visit, as if they had always been friends. The children were playing well together, and some of the older boys and girls were coyly eyeing each other. The marked difference in appearance of some of the Norge, having blond or red hair and blue or green eyes, seemed not to matter at all to the Mandan.

X

"Now, Grandson, you have heard the Ed-da from beginning to end. I don't believe that I left out anything of importance. Do you think you can recall most of it?"

"I am not sure, Grandfather; it is a very long story with many strange places and names. In time, if you will help me, I should be able to get it straight in my mind."

"Of course, I will help. It is important to me, if not to anyone else, that the story be kept alive."

"Do you have any questions concerning the Story?"

"I can't think of any right now, Grandfather, but I am sure that I will think of something later."

"Then, let me ask one of you. Now, think before you answer. Why do the People have four chiefs?"

"Well…you just got through telling me that the Mandan had two chiefs when the Norge joined them far down the Smoking River, one for the Missouri tribe and one for the…uh…others. What were the others called, Grandfather? I remember you said they were Lone Man's people, but was that their name? I suppose that after the villages combined, Steinn would have made three. The Mandan became one people made up of three tribes. Now there are the Mandan, Arikara, and Hidatsa. There are still three tribes and four chiefs. No, Grandfather I do not know why there are four."

"Grandson, you are a deep thinker. After Steinn joined the Mandan, they became one tribe made up of three different peoples, each with their own chief. A village with three chiefs becomes chaotic. When disputes arose that could not be settled because each faction wanted its own way, then a supreme ruler was needed to be chief over all. He is called the Wolf Chief; for like the wolf, he is leader of the whole pack, see? Even after the three tribes became as one, the tradition was continued. It must be a good system; it has worked for many generations."

"Now, about your question. The white race that was driven out of the valley of the Beautiful River joined with a portion of the Missouri tribe. These people were known as Welsh. They were also known as Modok's people. That is all that they knew about themselves, except that long ago they came from across the Sunrise Sea."

"What happened to the huge raft, Grandfather?"

"I can only guess that when it was no longer needed that the logs were used in the construction of the new lodges. What do you think?"

"That sounds reasonable. Have you never been curious enough to venture down the Smoking River to see if such a village ever existed or gone to the Red River to find the site of the very first village?"

"Yes, as a matter of fact, I have gone exploring far down the Smoking River, but not as far as the clear stream from the west. I went down one side and back up the other, and there are ruins of ancient villages in several places, but I have never gone very far to the east toward the Red River. For as long as I have lived, the Lakota have ruled the land to the east, and as you know, they have never been our close friends. We trade with them, but we have never been allies. Once, I followed an ancient bison trail over the hills, just there, on the east side of the Smoking River, to the headwaters of the Sheyenne River. It was the same trail, I believe, that the Norge used in coming to the river many, many years ago. Where we are sitting right now must not be very far from the place where Broken Hand's people crossed the river."

"The Story says that the Norge floated for eight days down the river, Grandfather. Why do we live here instead of far down the river?"

There are several reasons. As you should already know, after a number of years, our lodges, being made from wood and covered with earth, decay to the point where they cannot be repaired. Most of the trees in the vicinity of a village are eventually used up, and even though we mostly use bison dung as fuel, wood becomes a precious commodity. Also, for some reason the land where we plant our crops produces less each year. The whole community will then move to a new location where there are trees to build a new village, and there is soil that has never been tilled before. Why the movement has always been up the river? That I cannot say."

"Is there anything more that you wish to discuss, Grandson?

"No, I do not think so."

"Then we have talked enough for today. Run along and find your friends, and let an old man take a nap."

Wi had not yet risen above the horizon when Ninekiller settled into his favorite place at the log. He wriggled into the same formfitting spot in the ground as he had done countless times before. He chanted his prayers to the One God as the sun began to peek over the hills to the east across the river, then he included the sun also. Although he had worshiped the One God and His Son all his life, his reverence for the sun had never diminished. He believed that the One God had made man from the very ground he sat on, but he also believed that without the sun life would not exist on the earth.

Just as his prayers were finished, Ninekiller heard a long, plaintive whistle, announcing the coming of a riverboat up the river. He need not expect Ferret this morning, as he would be occupied until the afternoon. The arrival of a riverboat was a grand occasion to the Mandan. His people had always loved trading, and when the white man came with his woolen blankets and implements of steel, the Mandan became hooked. Some of the white man's goods made life much easier for the People, and had become indispensable, but he hated the liquid that burned the throat, called firewater by some, that took all dignity from a man. But what could one old man do to rectify the situation? The Mandan had become so dependent on the white man's products that it would be almost impossible for them to return to the old ways.

He couldn't see from his present position, but he knew that the People were already piling trade goods near the docking site. There would be piles of hides and mounds of cheap souvenir items made by the people to sell to the gullible *wasichu* who sometimes took passage on the riverboats just to see the sights. There were men and women in the village who would sell or trade anything they owned for the *wasichu* gold and firewater. Well, let them degrade themselves if they wished. Ninekiller didn't hate the white man; his religious beliefs allowed no room for hatred for anyone, but he hated what was happening to his people.

As for him, he had nothing to trade, and he had no desire for anything that might be aboard the boat. His one great regret was that Ferret was falling into the same trap as everyone else in the village, but he was young and might yet be saved. It would be up to him to try to steer the boy in the right direction. His son and daughter-in-law were already hopelessly snared and showed no sign of caring. He had tried to raise his son in the right way, but he had never been one to listen to sound advice, thinking his father was nothing more than an old killjoy who was out of touch with modern thinking.

Ninekiller wiled away the hours dozing in the warm sunshine, allowing his mind to wander where it would. His existence, now that he was too old to earn his way, was useless anymore; the only thing in his life that was worth holding onto was his Grandson. He loved that boy more than life itself, much more than he had ever loved his own son. He hated the fact that he could no longer contribute his share of the family's food supply. If he could hold onto life for maybe three more years, until the boy became old enough to make his own way, Nine Killer intended, late at night when no one was watching, to start walking south down the river or maybe west into the prairie, without food or weapon, never to return, and he hoped his body would never be found. He would rather his bones be picked clean by vultures than to have his son go through the pretence of mourning his passing.

He had had few friends in this life; he expected to have few in the next. The only one he looked forward to meeting in *Wanagi Yatu,* the Place of Souls, was Catkin, his beloved wife. If not for Ferret he would begin that final journey before the sun came up in the morning, but for the boy's sake he had to stay around a little longer.

Ninekiller, dozing in the warm sunshine, heard the faint sound of footsteps in the grass. He opened his eyes to see Ferret standing beside him, head hanging in sadness. The puppy, Ferret's constant companion, having doubled in size since the Story was begun, was chasing a butterfly from flower to flower.

"What is the matter, Grandson? Did you not enjoy the grand occasion?" he asked a little sarcastically.

"I had nothing to trade, Grandfather."

"Would your father not buy a sweet treat for you?"

"No…Father acted as if I was not even present. He…He had only one thought, or so it seemed. His only desire was for a container of the firewater. He and Mother drank the container empty before they tried to return to our lodge. They were staggering about, holding on to each other for support, until both of them, laughing with glee, fell into a heap in the dust of the street. I left them lying there unable to rise. Other people just pointed and laughed as they passed by. I suppose they are still there. A single tear began a slow journey down Ferret's cheek to hang from his chin. Ninekiller reached out his hand to bid his grandson to sit beside him. The boy sat down, and the old man clasped him to his chest. The tears began to flow more freely, falling into the old man's lap. Ninekiller's heart was in agony for his grandson; he felt nothing but disgust for his son and daughter-in-law.

Ninekiller knew that something momentous had occurred this day, other than the boy's parents getting drunk. They had done this very thing many times before. But he would not push his grandson. He would wait patiently until Ferret was ready to talk.

"Ordinarily, Grandfather, their antics would have been hilarious, but the method by which they purchased the firewater took all the humor out of it. Father and Mother, along with a horde of other people, pushed aboard the boat the instant it docked, even though the captain of the boat tried to prevent anyone from coming aboard, yelling that there was sickness there. The People crowded aboard anyway, despite the protests of the captain. I watched from the shore, afraid of being trampled, and besides, I had nothing to trade."

My father had nothing that the trader wanted either; you know all too well the work of my father's hands, and the man had already turned to walk away when Father whispered something in his ear. The trader turned and looked closely at Mother, from head to foot and back again, then called to another man nearby. That man came to stand beside the trader, and they exchanged words. The second man nodded his head before giving the trader a small yellow coin and taking my mother by the arm to lead her away. Father took the firewater offered by the trader and went ashore to wait for Mother to return."

"When Mother came hurrying ashore, she was laughing and reaching for the firewater. She took a swallow, then grimaced while shaking her head. Father took a drink and did the same thing. They both laughed hysterically and repeated the drinking ritual until the firewater was gone. I have already told you the rest of it. I have never been ashamed of my parents until this day. Why would they do such a thing, Grandfather?"

"Tomorrow, they too will be ashamed. They will be violently sick from the drinking and will be too ashamed to look us, or each other, in the eyes, but by the time another riverboat arrives, they will have forgotten the shame and probably do the same thing again. After a time, it becomes a sickness with people, completely ruining their lives. You are too young to have noticed, but there are others in this village that have given their lives to firewater. When this happens, the whole family suffers. If your mother and father do not change, they too will become slaves to this evil drink."

"I once tasted the awful stuff," Ninekiller continued. "The taste was disgusting. One must force oneself to swallow it. That is why your parents grimaced and shook their heads. Stay away from the awful drink, Grandson. It is a poison that slowly but surely destroys the drinker."

Ferret had stopped crying, and the old man thought that he had gone to sleep, but then the boy raised his head to look into his grandfather's eyes. "What can we do, Grandfather? How can we stop them from doing this thing again?"

"I am afraid there is nothing we can do except pray that the One God will intercede on their behalf. Your father has never been one to heed my advice. Because of my belief in the Norge tradition, my faith in the One God, and because I hold to the old ways of our people, he has never respected my opinions. Because of his laziness, his ineptitude, and his apparent lack of faith in anything at all, he in turn, has never earned my respect. Since we are so different, we have no rapport. It is a shame for father and son to be this way, but our relationship is not likely to change."

My life is nearly spent; it is you that I worry about, Grandson. But worrying accomplishes nothing. Today, let us put our troubles in the back of our minds. It will be some weeks before another riverboat arrives. This is the beginning of summer, a time to be joyful." For Ferret's sake, Ninekiller was putting on a front, a show of happiness he didn't feel in his own heart.

Two weeks had passed since the arrival of the riverboat, and as usual while the others in the lodge were still abed, Ninekiller was settling himself into his favorite spot at the log. As always, he finished his morning prayers just as the sun broke the horizon. Ferret, followed by the puppy, came to sit beside his grandfather. "I am hungry, Grandfather. Did you have anything to eat before you came out this morning?"

"No, Grandson. I thought maybe I would have something later. Is your mother not up yet?"

"Mother is not feeling well. She has a headache and a fever and is vomiting. Do you think that you could cook something for us? I think I could eat just about anything."

"All right. Let us go see what we can find to eat. If we cannot find anything we like, maybe we will use the hooks and line that I have had hidden away the whole winter to catch a few fish for breakfast. It will take a while to gather worms or grasshoppers for bait, and we must have a fishing pole, too. I have been waiting for just the right occasion to try the new hooks and line. They were ˙ irthday gift for you, but I feel today is the right time to present them to you. You will be amazed at how thin and strong this new string is. The People have nothing to compare with it. This is another *wasichu* product that will be very useful. All that I know about the new fishing line is what the *wasichu* trader told me. We will have to learn as we go."

"Why is the white man called *wasichu*, Grandfather? What does it mean?"

"It means the taker of fat. White men take the very best from the People and give as little as possible in return. Many of their trade items are cheap and inferior. It is a derogatory term that I should not be using, but it is true, nevertheless. In the future I shall try to refrain from using the term."

"For some reason, Grandfather, I am not as hungry as I was. I will take one of the *wasichu* metal cans and look for worms. I think I know exactly where to look. Where shall I meet you?"

"I will be at the spot where people throw trash into the Knife River. That should be a very good place to catch a catfish or two. I will see if I can find a fishing pole." Ninekiller smiled and shook his head as Ferret bounded away.

It took the old man longer to find a suitable pole than for Ferret to gather bait. The boy was waiting impatiently for his grandfather to arrive. In five minutes the pole was rigged, and Nine Killer threaded a worm onto the hook and showed Ferret how to swing the bait as far out as possible. He had no sooner handed the pole to Ferret than a large bream made for the bottom of the river with the bait deep in its mouth. Ferret was holding the pole too loosely and almost lost his grip as the fish pulled the tip of the pole into the water.

For days Ninekiller prayed every waking moment, but his prayers were to no avail as both his son and grandson were soon comatose. He carried water from the river to bathe the fevered bodies of the sick, but there was nothing else that could be done for them. People in the village were dieing right and left. The disease incapacitated whole families, and there was no one to care for them. They wallowed in their own filth until death brought blessed relief.

Looters were raiding the lodges of the sick, long before they died, carrying away items contaminated with lethal germs, not knowing that their greed would be the death of them.

Ninekiller could feel the disease slowly encroaching on his own body. He felt like crawling into bed and giving up, but there was a chance, however small, that his grandson might recover. He must somehow hold on a little longer. Ferret was now the Storyteller; he had to know if the boy would survive. If the One God really existed surely, he would save Ferret of all people to carry on His name.

The hours turned into days, and the old man, functioning by sheer will power, devoted his waning strength to the care of his son and grandson.

As the sun arose the next morning, Ninekiller could barely drag his much-weakened body to the bedside of his grandson. He felt Ferret's forehead, and his heart seemed to stop! The skin was cool to the touch! The realization that his grandson had died struck him like a great tree falling. His heart contracted with such force that he was sure that he, too, was going to die that instant, and he wanted it to happen. He waited a few seconds to see if he would lose consciousness, but when his heartbeat returned, he felt

Ferret's forehead again. There was no mistake; the boy was dead. The old man would have been relieved if he could have cried, but the hurt was too great. All he could do was moan like a wounded animal. His only reason for living was gone.

"Oh, One God, I have trained this little one to be the Storyteller in order to carry on your name, and now he is dead. Why have You allowed this to happen? From the time I was a child no older than Ferret I have believed in You and Your message of love and brotherhood, and I have lived according to Your teachings as best I knew how. Now, I realize that all my efforts have been in vain, and my waiting for Your return is to no avail. I have but a short time to live, and when I die, all knowledge of You will perish with me. There will be no one left to pray to You, to spread Your message to others. And if You do come again, there will be no one to receive You. I cannot understand why You have allowed this to happen."

"My life, all my effort on Your behalf, has been a total waste. Maybe the others were right all along. Maybe there was never any truth in the Story after all. My grandson wears the fish emblem as the symbol of the Storyteller, and for what reason? It is now all meaningless."

Ninekiller paused long enough to remove the emblem and steel arrowhead from Ferret's body. He crawled, expending the remainder of his strength, to the hearth in the center of the lodge. The fire had long gone out, and he did not have the strength to rekindle it, or he would have burned the two items. Instead, he scooped out a hole in the ashes and buried the fish emblem and arrowhead as deeply as possible. Fire would have had no effect on the stone and steel but burning them would have been an act of defiance, a symbol of his total disappointment in the One God.

"I fervently prayed for my grandson, and You did not hear; I refuse to pray for myself." With that said, the old man laid his head on his forearms and surrendered to the darkness.

As night fell a shadowy figure, after taking everything of value from the lodge, piled an armful of combustibles near the wall, and set it on fire. He then stealthily made his way to his own lodge, not realizing that he carried his own death in his arms.

Author's Notes

1. The western Greenland Colony disappeared in the mid 1300's. Evidence indicates that the inhabitants migrated to America.

2. In 1354, the King of Norway and Sweden commissioned Paul Knutson to go in search of the colonists. Nicholas of Lynn, Knutson's navigator returned to Norway, but Knutson did not.

3. Viking artifacts have been found along the Nelson River between Lake Winnipeg and Hudson Bay.

4. Boulders with triangular holes in them, called mooring stones, have been found in many places around the Great Lakes area.

5. A carved stone, the Kensington Rune Stone. Was found by a farmer in Minnesota in 1898.

6. When the first recorded white man, a Frenchman named Verendrye, visited the Mandan in 1734, he noted that many members of the tribe had Caucasian features, including blond or red hair, freckles, facial hair, and blue or green eyes.

7. The great earth houses and bullboats, or courigs, built by the Mandan were known to have been built in medieval Europe as well.

www.ingramcontent.com/pod-product-compliance
Lightning Source LLC
Chambersburg PA
CBHW021030130626
46552CB00005B/1775

* 9 781734 736236 *